PRAISE FOR
SHADOW WEAVER

★ "[Connolly's] use of language and suspense is captivating, resulting in a gripping tale that is wholly original. Dark, yet dazzling, this first installment in a planned duology is sure to be popular. A perfect choice for fans of Kelly Barnhill's *The Girl Who Drank the Moon*."

—*Booklist*, Starred Review

★ "*Shadow Weaver* is a spooky thriller filled with danger and magic… A fresh take on magic and friendship not to be missed."

—*Shelf Awareness*, Starred Review

"Fans of *Serafina and the Black Cloak* (2015) will find much the same chills and sequel-primed mystery here."

—*Kirkus Reviews*

"Vivid and invigorating."

—*School Library Journal*

"Connolly's narrative is full of meaningful moral lessons—on the limits of loyalty, the importance of honesty, and the absolute necessity of trusting others... An enchanting new juvenile fantasy series."

—*Foreword Reviews*

"This book contains plenty of action and intrigue to keep the reader turning pages. It is quick to read and contains enough unsolved mysteries to make the reader look forward to the next title in the series."

—*School Library Connection*

"The theme of friendship is handled deftly here... A gripping finale reveals the truth about the 'cure' for magic, and readers will eagerly anticipate learning more in a promised sequel."

—*Bulletin of the Center for Children's Books*

COMET RISING

ALSO BY MARCYKATE CONNOLLY

Shadow Weaver

COMET RISING

MarcyKate Connolly

sourcebooks
jabberwocky

Published by Sourcebooks Jabberwocky, an imprint of Sourcebooks, Inc.
P.O. Box 4410, Naperville, Illinois 60567-4410
(630) 961-3900
Fax: (630) 961-2168
sourcebooks.com

Library of Congress Cataloging-in-Publication Data
Names: Connolly, MarcyKate, author.
Title: Comet rising / MarcyKate Connolly.
Description: Naperville, Illinois : Sourcebooks Jabberwocky, [2019] | Sequel
to: Shadow weaver. | Summary: Emmeline and her best friend
Lucas, a light singer, must try to use their powers to stop evil Lady
Aisling, the magic eater, once and for all.
Identifiers: LCCN 2018010652 | (hardcover : alk. paper)
Subjects: | CYAC: Magic--Fiction. | Shadows--Fiction. | Fantasy.
Classification: LCC PZ7.1.C64685 Com 2019 | DDC [Fic]--dc23 LC record available at
https://lccn.loc.gov/2018010652

Source of Production: Maple Press, York, Pennsylvania, United States
Date of Production: November 2018
Run Number: 5013506

Printed and bound in the United States of America.
MA 10 9 8 7 6 5 4 3 2 1

For my family.

CHAPTER ONE

I have not cast a shadow in two months, three days, and eleven hours. There is nothing tethered to my feet, no one imitating my every move, no one whispering in my ear. Everything else around me does cast one, and I can scoop them up and mold them with my shadowcraft. It is only me who has to go without her constant companion. I never fully understood what it was like to be alone until now.

My shadow, Dar, resides upstairs, locked in the attic in a cage of shadow and light. It is safer that way.

This morning, my best friend Lucas and I have been practicing our talents on the beach below our cliff-side cottage while his parents tend to their garden. Talents like Lucas's light singing and my shadow weaving are rare and only bless children once every twenty-five years when the Cerelia Comet soars through the night sky. We were hunted in our previous home in Parilla, but here in Abbacho, Lady Aisling—the woman who wishes to steal our magic and my shadow—cannot reach us.

At least, not yet.

A few weeks ago, we mastered fishing with light hooks and shadow ropes. Lucas's parents let us catch all the fish now and our icebox is already full, though it's not even midday. So, Lucas is practicing skipping light over the water, turning it into discs that move like stones but never sink. I sit in the sand with my legs outstretched and ankles crossed, laughing while he makes the light shimmy and dance with his song. There are not as many shadows here in Abbacho compared to where I grew up. My first home was filled with trees and hidden nooks, but here, next to the ocean, the sun is always high overhead and the trees are thinner.

I have learned to improvise.

The ocean contains more shadows than one might think. Those cast by reefs and seaweed and even the little shadows cast by fish braving the shallows are mine for the taking. This morning I've exhausted myself trying to pull them from deeper waters. The ocean is vast, and I can feel the darkness lurking under the waves like someone breathing down my neck. Something about the water seems to dull my call too, so practicing takes more out of me than pulling shadows through the air. But every day I get a little better.

"Lucas! Emmeline!" Miranda calls from the top of the cliff. "You'd better bring in your catch. It's almost time for lunch."

Together, we lift the icebox and carry it up the winding footpath to the cottage. When we walk in the door, Miranda already has the fixings for sandwiches set out on the table, just waiting for Lucas to arrive and toast the bread. But before we've even set down our catch, a terrible scream echoes through the house, rattling my bones.

"What on earth is Dar up to now?" Miranda says, glancing uneasily at the ceiling.

I quickly put together a sandwich and trudge up the stairs. The wailing continues, growing more piercing by the minute.

I pause to take a deep breath before opening the attic door. It's always best to brace myself before facing Dar. At least we have no neighbors to complain about the noise. Sometimes I wonder what my parents would think if they could see Dar now. They never did believe she was real when she was just my shadow.

When I enter the little attic room, I nearly drop the tray with Dar's sandwich. It's the same as I left it this morning—plain and sparse, with fresh daffodils in a vase on the table by the window that looks out on the sea. But Dar is different. Usually, she plays coy and mimics me as I enter, then begs and pleads to be released.

But I did not expect this.

Dar is wearing my shape today, as she often does, but something is off. She has worn her fingernails to the nub scratching at the bars of her shadow-and-light cage. Her hair is disheveled, and a thin line of blood trickles down her forehead onto her right cheek, almost like she's been banging her head against the bars. Now she sits in one corner of the cage, clutching her knees to her chest and rocking back and forth, wailing like something out of a nightmare.

"Dar." I keep my voice as steady as possible while I slip the sandwich tray through the bars. "What happened?"

She stops her wailing and stares at me like she's seen a ghost. Fear slithers down my neck, but I shake it off. Dar lunges, tears streaming unchecked, and I step back. She has tried every argument possible to convince me to release her from the cage.

Could this be another trick? She seems truly distressed. But she deceived me for so long I can't trust myself to tell for certain.

It's unnerving to see her behave like this while wearing my face. Some days she shifts into Miranda, Lucas, Alfred, or one of the strange creature shapes she loved when she was a shadow. But she always returns to me, my shape. I suspect it feels a little like home.

"Emmeline," Dar says hoarsely. "It's happening." She scratches at her face and then shudders.

"What do you mean? What is happening?"

Her brow creases and more tears spill over her cheeks. "Can't you feel it? The shiver in your bones, creeping into your skin, tingling with power?" She scratches her forearm, and I realize scrapes cover her hands, neck, and face. "It makes me itchy."

"I'm sorry, Dar, but I don't feel anything like that." My former shadow has been a handful ever since I made her flesh again. Guilt twinges in my chest. Being locked in the attic may have something to do with that, but it is too risky to set her loose. If free, she will take her revenge on Lady Aisling—her sister—without any care for the destruction she might leave in her wake.

"Oh, but you will. And soon. It's coming." Clutching the bars, Dar gazes out the window as if she fears someone is sitting just outside waiting to pounce.

She's baiting me, but I can't deny I'm curious. "What is coming, Dar?"

"The comet," she whispers.

I frown. "The comet? Not the—"

"Yes! The Cerelia Comet."

"That's impossible. It passes by once every twenty-five years. It's only been thirteen since the last time."

Fear flashes in Dar's eyes. "It's Lady Aisling. It has to be. It is the only explanation." She scratches at her neck. "She did something. She brought it back early to have more children to plant in her garden and harvest at her leisure."

I recoil. Lady Aisling is pure evil. She is a magic eater. From her estate in Zinnia, she sends out hunters to gather up talented children under the guise of curing them. Then she transforms them into flowers, keeping them alive in her Garden of Souls so she can steal their powers whenever she pleases. She's the reason Lucas's family and I are in hiding. She wants my talent and Lucas's too. And she wants her sister back.

She is the one thing that scares me more than Dar being set free, and Dar knows it. This must be a trick. A big one. Dar must have been planning it for some time.

I fold my arms across my chest. "That is impossible, and you know it. No one can change a comet's path."

"Are you sure?" Dar says. "What if there's a talent out there that could?"

I shiver, but my glare doesn't waver. "I highly doubt that."

Dar pushes her face against the shadow-and-light bars. "You must let me out. Please, Emmeline. This is too important. I know Lady Aisling, and I am the only one who can stop her. You must set me free right now."

And there it is. That is all she wants. Everything else she says or does is just a lie. Well, she fooled me for years. I won't let her do it again. I'm no longer the naive girl who ran away from home so many months ago.

"Nice try, Dar." I head for the door. "Keep it down in here, all right?"

"No! Emmeline, you must listen. The comet is coming *tonight*! I swear I'm telling the truth. I felt it before when I was just a shadow. Now that I'm human again, it's even stronger."

I shake my head. She looks pitiful in that cage. If I didn't know better, I might believe her.

"I'm not letting you out, and that's final."

I close the door behind me, and Dar's shrieks follow me down the stairs. "It's coming! It's coming!"

Even though I know it is not true, I pull all the shadows in the stairway around me like a cloak for comfort. Just in case.

CHAPTER TWO

L ater that evening, when dusk begins to fall, I linger outside longer than usual, soaking up the shadows. Dar's words have stuck with me all day, tiny barbs I cannot pluck off. After I told Lucas and his parents what she said, Lucas offered to bring Dar her supper tonight in my place. Now, I'm out here enjoying my shadows, thin wisps of smoke circling my arms and weaving through my hair like ribbons. They dodge and twirl at my command, always playful and pleased to have some of my attention. The day may belong to Lucas, but the night is all mine.

Lucas opens the front door and shakes his golden head at me. I sigh. "I take it her dinner went well?"

"About as well as you'd expect." He shrugs. "She was mad I wasn't you at first, but then she tried the same story on me."

We make our way down to the beach. The moon is rising in the sky, and it lights our path. When we hit the sand, we break into a run, the sea breeze whipping my hair as I collect shadows around me. Lucas pulls bits of starlight into an orb that hovers over our heads to complement the moonlight.

Where the cliff meets the ocean, the water retreats at low tide, revealing a strip of sand and rocks that leads to ocean caves usually hidden by the waves. We make our way quickly, knowing the tide will come in faster than we'd like. It isn't long before the caves appear. We have yet to explore them all, but one is our favorite: it's more of a nook, but it has sides worn smooth and provides the perfect spot for us to sit and watch the stars at night or the gulls swoop and play during the day.

We scramble inside our cave and sit, tucking our legs beneath us. Lucas's orb floats to the back and settles. He pulls out a handful of taffies and offers one to me. I savor it while we watch the rest of the stars come out. The darkness under the waves is stronger at night, and the pull here is magnetic. I cannot help but stare, mesmerized by the ocean crashing a few yards away from us.

"Do you think she's right?" Lucas says after a while. Something tickles my arm, and I scratch it absentmindedly.

"Of course not. It's just another lie." I sigh, glancing with a pang of jealousy at Lucas's shadow. "Everything she says is a lie."

"Something seemed different this time." Lucas rubs his ear.

"No. She never changes. I don't think she ever will." And that is the trouble with Dar. We had hoped she might calm down after spending some time locked up, but it has only made her wilder. We have yet to decide what to do about her, though I know Miranda and Alfred discuss the subject when they think we're asleep. Even without Dar by my side, I haven't fully shed my habit of eavesdropping. It really is the best way to find out important things the adults don't want you to know.

My cheek twinges and I scratch it. I call more shadows to me and craft them into a soft cushion. We settle onto it and fall into a reassuring silence as we watch the waves and the stars together. It's peaceful here, and after the spectacle of the afternoon, it's what I need most. Lucas senses it.

Another itch pinches my calf, and I scratch that too. I frown.

"Emmeline!" Lucas cries. I look in the direction he points, sucking my breath in sharply enough that my chest aches.

Something brilliant sails across the night sky—pure white light, almost like one of Lucas's orbs, with a long tail that sparkles like stardust trailing after it. As it passes over, tiny specks of light fall to the earth, dusting the ocean and the forest far beyond.

I cannot move even though my entire body is on fire, like a thousand mosquitoes have bitten me all at once.

The Cerelia Comet has returned.

CHAPTER THREE

iranda and Alfred insist Lucas and I go to bed immediately after we run back inside, shaking like leaves. Dar howls upstairs, but after Miranda gives her a stern talking-to, she settles down. I don't know whether they believe us, but I lay in my bed while curiosity consumes me from the inside out.

In the past, Dar would wrap her shadowed form around me and whisper in my ear, goading me to sneak about and find out more.

Don't you want to know, Emmeline? Just listen for a few minutes and then we can go back to bed...

I can't help it. I slide the covers off and set my feet on the cool floor. The shadows lurking in the room flock to me as I make my way out into the hall. This is not the first time I have done this without Dar, but I can't help feeling like something is missing. I tiptoe to the door of the kitchen and peek around the corner, my shadows camouflaging me in the dark. Miranda and Alfred stand over the kitchen table, which is littered with papers. Miranda's hair has slipped out of her usual braid and floats around her face, twisting with every gesture she makes. Alfred frowns so hard his glasses keep sliding down the bridge of his nose.

"If the comet has truly returned early, it can only be a bad omen," Miranda says. "Something powerful had to have pulled it from its usual path to make this happen."

Alfred pushes his glasses back up his nose. "That should be impossible."

Miranda slaps her hand on the table and the papers jump. "No, it isn't, and you know it." She picks a scroll off the table and holds it up. "See? Right here."

"That was two hundred years ago. There haven't been any reports of a sky shaker in our lifetime."

Miranda huffs. "Well, there haven't been shadow weavers

and light singers in a long time either, but here they are under our roof."

Alfred looks like he just swallowed something unpleasant. "That's a fair point. But a sky shaker would know better. The risks of moving something like a comet into a new path are too great."

"A sky shaker might know better, but not Lady Aisling. Not if she stood to benefit," Miranda says.

"We need to inform the rest of the network immediately. We should go to the village tomorrow. The others need to know. This change in the comet's path could mean danger for us all."

"And we need to be ready." Miranda rolls up the scroll and tucks it into a drawer. I make a mental note. I have seen that scroll before. I didn't know what to make of it at the time, but ever since Miranda and Alfred told us about the network of talented folks, I've understood: it's a list of the names, dates of birth, and locations of every known comet-blessed person. We all keep tabs on one another and help one another move around before Lady Aisling and her hunters come knocking.

Of course, Miranda and Alfred don't know that I know all

of this. This is why they sent us to bed early. They don't want us to be any more frightened than we already are. And they didn't want us to know about the possibility of a sky shaker. I've never heard of one, but it must be a fearsome talent if it can move a comet into a new path.

I shiver as Alfred's words ring in my ears. What danger could the Cerelia Comet's new path bring?

Miranda and Alfred embrace, and he kisses the top of her head. He puts away the papers while Miranda tidies up the kitchen. I wait a few beats more just to be sure nothing else interesting is going to be said, then tiptoe back to my room.

I wish I had someone to share my newfound knowledge with, but Dar is out of the question, and Lucas might not look kindly on my eavesdropping on his parents. Instead, I lie awake, their words circling my brain in an endless loop. But it does not lull me to sleep; with every repetition the icy fear that settled at the base of my spine the moment I saw the Cerelia Comet seeps into my veins.

Dar was right. I know it in my bones. Lady Aisling has done something. Something terrible.

And she is coming for us next.

←—•—→

The next morning when I wake, my shadows are wrapped tightly around me despite the sun shining in through the windows. I don't want to let them go. With a sigh I return them to their homes and dress quickly. Lucas's parents said something about going to the village, and I don't want to miss out.

When I reach the kitchen, Lucas is already at the table with his family, digging into breakfast. Miranda puts eggs on my plate and hands me the platter of toast. Miranda and Alfred are always warm and informal, so very different from my own parents. If I didn't eat with the right fork, my mother would scold me, but here I could eat with my fingers, and Lucas's parents wouldn't even blink. I walked on eggshells all the time with my parents, but here I finally feel like I belong. It feels like home.

"We're going to the village this morning," Miranda says. "We have an important meeting, but you and Lucas can explore the market on your own."

"Who are you meeting?" I ask innocently, but quickly shut my mouth at Miranda's stern expression.

"Don't feel bad," Lucas says. "I asked her the same thing."

I smile at him and polish off my breakfast. Lucas is as curious about the network as I am. But his light can't give him the knowledge my darkness can.

Soon we head for the village. I miss the old cottage in Parilla. The trip to the village there was full of trees and shadows, even on sunny days. But here it's nothing but sparse grass and trees that are tall and spindly and spaced apart. Their wide leaves make odd shadows here and there. I twirl a couple on my fingers, letting them circle my wrists and make their way up my arms. With a snap of my fingers, they pull my hair back from my face, fastening it in a neater bow than I could ever tie with my own hands.

Beside me, Lucas toys with sparks of light, but as we get close, his parents stop us. "Emmeline, put away your shadows. Lucas, leave the light alone." While Abbacho is supposed to be safe, it's best our talents remain hidden.

The village is homey and friendly, and most of the villagers have already learned our names. As far as they're concerned, I am Lucas's sister, and we are a family of farmers and fishers who live along the coast. Our secrets have not been guessed, and hopefully they never will.

The houses are crafted from stone and wood, with slanted slate roofs. Most are shades of the seashore—tan beach sands, creamy ocean foam dotted with deep blues and greens. Sometimes the salty scent of the sea wafts by on the wind, even stronger when it rains. Today the sky threatens overhead, churning grays and casting shadows from the buildings and the people every which way. It's just the sort of day I love best. And so did Dar.

I swallow the pang of loss as we wander into the village. People smile at us in greeting, and when we get to the market square, I've begun to relax. Everything here is normal. Still, I glance warily at the sky, remembering Alfred's words about the comet from the night before.

We run freely through the crowd, though with strict instructions to return to the entrance in one hour. We make a beeline for the baker's cart that sells sticky buns and chocolate tarts. Miranda and Alfred disappear into the throng before we even turn around.

Lucas frowns as he takes a bite of his treat. "What do you think their meeting is all about?"

I bite my tongue before answering. "Maybe it has something to do with the comet?"

His eyes flash. "It must. I wish they'd let us help. Our talents are not for nothing, you know." He kicks a stone in front of him in frustration.

I take a deep breath. "Well," I say. "We could follow them. If you wanted to. Just to see what they're up to." I glance away quickly. "Or not. It was just a thought." I don't want Lucas to think me bad, but he seems to be as curious as I am.

He does not scold me. Instead, his face breaks into a sly grin. "Can you hide us in your shadows?"

I nearly laugh out loud. Last night, I was concerned what he'd think of me for spying on his parents, and now here he is suggesting the very same thing. Somehow that makes me feel a little less guilty.

"Of course I can. It's a gloomy enough day that no one will notice an extra shadow bouncing around. Come on." I motion toward an empty stall and we duck behind it. Then I call the shadows from carts and banners and the people forming the crowd and mold them into a hazy blanket. No one can see us behind it. Or at least most people can't. I shudder, remembering Simone. Poor girl. She's a mind reader, stolen by Lady Aisling and turned into a shell of a person. The girl is in there still somewhere, but the Lady controls her most of the time. She could see through my shadows by sensing my mind behind them.

Before we can move away from the stall, two women stop in front of it, blocking our way. We have no choice but to wait a few minutes more. We may not catch up to his parents if we don't leave now. But the conversation the women are having quickly becomes interesting.

"What do you think they were here for, Marcella?" the youngest asks. They speak in whispers.

The older woman takes the girl's arm. "I can't imagine. The Lady knows her men are not welcome in Abbacho. But John swears he saw them camped only a few miles from here just last night. I suppose it might have something to do with that comet."

"Let's hope they're not headed this way," the girl says, a frown marring her pretty face. "I've heard they're all brutes."

Marcella harrumphs. "When we get home, I shall write to our local magistrate to complain. We don't want their kind around here. The Lady loves to meddle, from what I understand, and we don't need her doing that in Abbacho, that's for certain."

Marcella takes the girl's arm and leads her away, cautiously looking over her shoulder as though Lady Aisling's hunters might be coming for them.

I don't realize my hands are shaking until Lucas covers them with his own. "We'll tell my parents and they'll know what to do." His face brightens. "And maybe this time they'll let us help."

I try to smile, but I don't feel reassured. If Lady Aisling's men are here, they're searching for us and Dar. She'll never stop, and there is only so far we can run.

"Besides," Lucas says. "We defeated her men last time. You were brilliant. I'm sure we can do it again if we must."

That reminder does make me feel a little better. We finally leave the stall and head in the direction Lucas's parents took. We wander through the crowds, keeping to the shadows on the sides, past the brightly painted signs and smells of the food vendors. When we reach the edge of the market, we are just in time to see Miranda and Alfred coming out from the back of a shop with a sign out front that says Closed. We stop.

"Why is that shop closed in the middle of the day?" Lucas whispers.

"So that no one will come in and accidentally overhear

what they were discussing with your parents." I etch the shop into my memory. The sign says ALSA'S APOTHECARY and it's painted a dark blue with pale blue shutters. The blinds are drawn.

Lucas tugs on my hand. "We should get back to our meeting spot before they realize we were following them."

We hurry back as quickly as we can. "I'm sorry we didn't get to follow them into the shop, Lucas. I know we both wanted to hear what they had to say."

"And see who they were meeting with," Lucas grumbled. "It isn't fair that they keep so much from us. We've fought off Lady Aisling's men. That should count for something."

I can't help but agree. Haven't we done enough to prove we're a part of this fight?

But try explaining that to Miranda and Alfred and you'd think we were asking them to fly to the moon.

"Lucas, I may have overheard something last night. About the comet."

Curiosity is aflame in his eyes. "Something my parents said?"

"They mentioned a sky shaker. They seemed worried that it might be dangerous for the comet to be on a new path." My hands are sweaty. I twist them in my skirts.

Lucas's eyes widen. "Dangerous? What do you mean?"

"I don't know. They didn't say anything specific. But they said it was important for the network to know."

He remains thoughtful as we narrowly dodge a group of giggling schoolchildren. I'm grateful he doesn't ask me how I heard these things, though I'm sure he's guessed. We round one last corner and we're back at the meeting spot with time to spare. We duck into the unused stall, and I release my shadows wistfully.

We creep out just in time to greet Lucas's parents. Their faces are long and drawn, and my heart takes a seat in my throat. Whatever they discovered, it did not make them happy.

Lucas's mother embraces us both in greeting. "It's time to go home."

"Well?" Lucas says. "What did you find out?"

"You know better than to ask that," Alfred admonishes, and Lucas's hopeful face falls. We walk in silence the rest of the way home.

CHAPTER FOUR

Dinner is a quiet affair, and afterward Lucas and I are shuffled off to bed faster than usual. Miranda and Alfred clearly wish to speak freely without us present. Dar has gone sullen too. She barely said two words to me when I brought up her meal. Instead, she sat in the corner of her cage and stared at me.

I find her silence even more disconcerting than her dramatic predictions.

When I climb into bed, I can't shake the feeling something is out there, looming over my shoulder just waiting for the right time to pounce.

Sleep does not come easy. Through the door, I can hear the

murmur of Miranda and Alfred's conversation in the kitchen. I desperately want to listen in, but tonight it feels more wrong than last night. Like it would be directly disobeying their wishes.

Eventually I fall into a half-waking dream of flowers and ladies and lost powers, when something startles me awake. A keening from upstairs.

Dar is at it again. Frustrated, I throw off the covers and put on my slippers. I've never owned a pet, but I suspect this is what having to care for one is like. Shadows are generally quite well behaved, with Dar being the notable exception. I suppose that's what I get for making her flesh again.

I take a step toward my bedroom door, but as I pass the window, I stop in my tracks. Something is out of place. I peer into the night. There are only a couple sparse trees waving in the wind. Otherwise, it is mostly long grasses stretching from the cliff's edge to the wooded area farther away. But I swear I just saw a shadow move in the yard—and not one called by me.

From here I can see all the way down to the beach below the cliff. My breath stutters in my chest. There are many shadows swarming there—shadows made by men. The one I glimpsed in the field must be a scout.

Dar must have seen them too.

My pulse pounds in my temple, and I rush from my room, throwing up a shadow to conceal me as I go. I duck into Lucas's room, and it takes a moment for me to shake him awake.

"Lucas!" I hiss. "We have to flee. Lady Aisling has found us."

His eyes fly open despite his grogginess. "Get Dar. I'll warn my parents."

I don't hesitate. The attic stairs fly under my feet two at a time until I'm at the top, fumbling with the key around my neck. Dar's keening has grown louder and more persistent. With shaking hands, I manage to unlock the door.

Within her cage, Dar has shrunk down to the size of a mouse. She sits at the bottom with her arms wrapped around her knees. She gazes up at me—still wearing my face—with red, teary eyes. "Please don't leave me here for them to find. If you won't release me, then shrink the cage, Emmeline, and take me with you." She sobs. "Please."

There is no time to waste. I don't want her to fall into Lady Aisling's hands any more than she does. I make the cage tighter, smaller, more condensed until it fits around her tiny form snugly. Now she and her cage can fit in my satchel and no one will know.

As long as she stays quiet, of course.

I pick up the cage and whisper to her, "I'm going to put you in my bag. No crying, no wailing, no talking. Not until we're safe, all right?"

Dar only nods in response. I hurry back down the stairs with a shadow curled around me. Miranda is in the kitchen yanking open drawers and tucking papers into her own bag. Some lay strewn about the floor, and she curses softly not realizing I'm there. One scroll in particular catches my eye. It's the one she and Alfred argued over just the other night. Lucas and his father reach the kitchen as I let my shadows down.

"I'll surround us all in darkness. Then they won't see any of us while we flee," I say, but Miranda firmly shakes her head.

"No, we're surrounded on all sides. We can't slip between them easily. Alfred and I will create a distraction so you can sneak away. You're too important. You can't fall into Lady Aisling's hands." She thrusts a bunch of papers toward Lucas. "Take these. They're our files for the network. Keep them safe. If we get caught, at least she won't have all of them. Go and wait for us in the village at Alsa's Apothecary. She can be trusted and will keep you hidden until we can join you."

Lucas's face is aghast. "You mean you're not coming with us?"

Alfred places a hand on his son's shoulder. "Of course we are. But we need to be sure you two can escape first. You must go on ahead. With Emmeline's shadows you will be safe."

"But who will keep you safe?" Lucas says.

Miranda shakes her head. "Even if Lady Aisling does capture us, what is she going to do? We have no magic for her to steal. It's worth the risk to ensure your safety."

"But we need you," Lucas says. "How will we access the network without you? We don't even know where to begin looking since you've barely told us anything!"

"Find Alsa. She will help you," Alfred says.

"Now go. They get closer with every second you waste," Miranda says.

One glance out the window confirms she's right. Dark figures surround us on all sides now, more joining them every minute. I scoop up more papers—including the scroll I recognized—and stuff them on top of Dar's cage, then grab Lucas's hand, ready to drag him from the cottage if necessary. I am loath to leave behind his parents, but I understand their logic.

There is too much at stake for me and Lucas to risk being caught. It would mean a half-life transformed into a flower in the Lady's garden at best or at worst becoming a living puppet like Simone.

Miranda and Alfred embrace us in quick succession then throw open the back door. They race off in opposite directions, leaving the way to the forest clear. I send two small shadows with them, directing one to stick with Miranda, and the other to remain with Alfred. With any luck, it will fool the guards long enough to make them believe they each have one of us with them.

The guards give chase, and Lucas and I slip out the front door under the cover of my shadows, racing down the dirt path toward the cliff and the woods. As we run I weave more shadows into a dozen human shapes about our size. Then I set them free in all directions with orders to keep moving, keep running, until dawn.

That ought to give them plenty to chase after.

We move as fast as our feet will carry us around the cliff's edge. The dark shapes of Lady Aisling's men move in single file along the base of the cliff to avoid the crashing, foaming waves of high tide. My heart lurches into my throat. There are so many. Far more than were sent to hunt us through the woods of Parilla.

I don't see how Miranda and Alfred can possibly escape. The soldiers swarm up the cliff-side path like a green ribbon, hard on their heels. By the time we reach the tree line, I know they've both been caught. We crouch down between the trees, Lucas shivering beside me despite the warm air. His eyes are wide and watery. I clutch his hand and squeeze. My shadows protect us from the soldiers' view.

"We should attack," Lucas whispers. "We have to do something. We can't just leave them."

"But they insisted we do exactly that. If we attack, we risk being caught too. There are too many."

A muffled voice pipes up from within my bag. "Run! Emmeline, please." I set her cage in my palm. Dar pleads, clutching the bars between her tiny hands. "Lady Aisling knows your powers and how they work. You can count on her preparing her men with something that can thwart you both."

I shudder, but Lucas frowns. "You're a liar and a coward. We don't need to take your advice on anything."

But Dar doesn't respond. Instead she gazes past him, horror-struck. She begins to shake, her mouth flapping open and shut like a bird trying to take flight. I glance in the direction she stares and see a new figure in a long, dark green cloak. It is clearly not a soldier.

"It's her," Dar finally manages to whisper.

My head snaps back to Dar. "What?"

"Lady Aisling. She's here."

Every nerve freezes, washing my body in cold.

Dar begs with renewed vigor. "You have to run, Emmeline. Or let me out. I'll take her on for you. Yes, that would be even better." She shakes again, this time transforming into a tiny version of her favorite monster shape.

"Absolutely not," I say.

"Then run," Dar says. "You can't risk it."

"But what about my parents?" Lucas says. They both give me pleading eyes. I cannot see Lady Aisling's face, but she seems to float eerily over the ground with a presence that commands respect.

Indecision freezes me to the ground. Soldiers approach, and two figures are dropped at the Lady's feet: Miranda and Alfred, hands tied behind their backs.

"No," Lucas whispers, his shoulders slumping.

We have no choice now but to save ourselves. They risked themselves to give us time to get away, and we've been wasting it. I get to my feet and put Dar back in my bag.

"Come on, Lucas," I say softly. "I'm sorry. We have to go. Right now."

His eyes water, but he gets to his feet. Together we run, guiltily leaving behind the only people who have ever protected us to face the wrath of Lady Aisling alone.

CHAPTER FIVE

The sound of braying horses in the distance follows us as we flee to the local village. We have a head start at the very least. But this time, I do not have Dar watching my back. A tiny part of me can see how useful she might be if we let her out, but it isn't worth the risk.

There's no telling the havoc she might wreak.

When we reach the village gates, we slip through unnoticed thanks to my shadows. And we stay hidden all the way to the back door of the blue building we saw Miranda and Alfred use earlier today. Tonight the building is cloaked in shadows just like we are, almost like it's hiding. I take a deep breath, then I release my shadows and knock.

It takes a few moments—long enough to make me wonder if we should just run—but the door finally creaks open. A tall woman—Alsa, presumably—with pale hair and big round glasses gazes down at us as she pulls her robe more tightly against the chilly night air.

"If you need an elixir, come back in the morning. And use the front entrance. We're closed now." She begins to shut the door.

"Wait! Please," I say. "Miranda and Alfred told us to come here for help." I lower my voice. "They've been taken by Lady Aisling."

The woman's expression changes, and she opens the door wide. "Get inside before anyone else sees you." She locks the door behind her.

Alsa leads us into a warm kitchen in the living quarters behind her storefront and directs us to take a seat at the table. The place is homey and neat, like she had just finished cleaning up for the night when we knocked. "Tell me everything," she says.

Lucas has grown quiet beside me, so I quickly relay the events of the past hour. Her scowl deepens with every word. When I finish, she gets to her feet and begins rifling through a nearby cabinet.

"Lady Aisling has been causing trouble for a very long time." She clicks her tongue disapprovingly. "Most folks without talents just assume she's an eccentric noblewoman from another territory. They have no idea that she steals children, because she's gotten craftier over the years. She's careful to cover her tracks. But to abduct your parents when they don't have talents? Well, that's just spiteful, now isn't it?"

"How long, exactly, has she been doing this?" I ask. "Do you know?" This is a thing I have long wondered. Dar isn't sure how old she really is, or how long she spent as a shadow. Time passes differently in the shadow world, apparently.

Alsa raises her eyebrows. "Now that is a mighty good question. Longer than any normal person has a right to live, that's for certain. The first record we have of her stealing a talent is one hundred years ago."

I gasp. "How is that possible?" My mind reels from the revelation of how old Lady Aisling—and Dar—must be. I can't even imagine it. She has had decades to perfect her talent; how can we hope to win against her?

"A lot is possible when you have any talent you desire. At some point, she must have acquired a life bringer. Someone who can heal others and bring them back from the brink of death. And to stay young, she must have a youth keeper too. Her garden is full of the most coveted talents. The sheer size of it was enough to impress the Zinnian nobles and convince them she's a noble herself. She wasn't born high, mind you. Her title of Lady is just airs she puts on, aided by her trove of magic." Alsa sighs. "You can spend the night here in my safe room. But you'll want to leave at dawn. The village will be the first place the hunters search for you."

I frown. "But where should we go? Miranda and Alfred told us we should stay here and wait."

"That, my dear, was before they got caught. This changes everything." She places an old book on the table between us and flips through until she lands on the section she wants. The writing is in a tiny hand, and the ink is faded on the yellowing pages.

"I met with Miranda and Alfred yesterday. They told me about the comet returning early. A sky shaker is the only reasonable explanation."

"Lady Aisling must have stolen their talent."

Alsa gives me a shrewd glance. "Aye. It's been a long time since a sky shaker has been around. They are among the rarest of talents. And dangerous. It is troubling for Lady Aisling to have one, let alone have the gall to use their magic."

"How are they dangerous?" I ask.

"They can move anything in the sky wherever they want it. The sun, the moon, the stars, or in this case, comets."

"But why is that so dangerous?"

"Think of it this way: Everything in the heavens is already in perfect alignment. The sun shines when we need it to, the moon comes out to light our way at night, the stars twinkle when they should. And that comet flies by every twenty-five years. Now, move one of those things out of its regular path, and it might get in the way of the others. It could throw the skies above completely off-kilter."

I'm still not clear why this is terrible, and it must show on my face. Alsa sighs, but, before she can respond, Lucas speaks. "If the sun doesn't shine when it should, plants won't grow. If they don't grow, we won't have food."

"Precisely. Also, there are other celestial bodies like meteors that can be thrown off course too, which means they might fall and damage our lands. Without careful planning and consideration, a new sky shaker could be dangerous." She points to the book in front of her. "One such event was recorded in our histories here. A sky shaker fell in love with a noblewoman and wanted to prove his devotion. He moved several stars into a new constellation just for her, making navigation difficult for those who relied on the stars to guide them. Then, she rejected him for another suitor." Alsa closes the book and leans back in her chair, folding her arms across her chest. "The sun didn't shine for two weeks until his closest friend managed to talk some sense into him and got him to put the skies back into their proper alignment."

Lucas's eyes are wide, horror-struck at the prospect of no sunlight for that long. But I can only think of how much I'd love to be safe in the darkness for more than just a few precious hours each day.

"That's horrible," Lucas says.

"It is," agrees Alsa. "Which is why we need to find the sky shaker."

"But if Lady Aisling has captured them, she isn't just going to let them go," I say.

A grim expression crosses Alsa's face. "No, she's not. She brought the comet around early to have more talents to harvest.

The older generations of talented folks have all disappeared, either long dead or planted in her garden. They didn't have the network to warn and hide them like we do now. She certainly isn't going to just release a newly acquired talent. We'll have to find a way to free them so that they can set the heavens right again before it's too late."

"How do you know all this?" I ask, feeling bolder than usual.

Alsa cracks a smile. "Have Miranda and Alfred told you much about the network?"

We nod, neglecting to mention they haven't told us very much at all. We don't want to risk her clamming up.

"I'm the historian. That's why they came to me. We haven't seen a sky shaker in ages, and they wanted to be sure they understood the ramifications. I was going to leave in the morning in search of a talent that could help."

I sit up straighter. "We could come with you. Maybe we could help?"

Alsa considers, scratching her chin. "Well, I'm not as young as I used to be. And I don't have a talent. My daughter was the talented one."

"Was?" Lucas says.

Alsa's face darkens. "Yes. Until Lady Aisling stole her. At least, I believe she did. It was years ago that she went missing. That's when I joined the network. I don't want any other parents to have to suffer the same fate." She stands up. "But without magic, I might be a liability. I know about your talents—Miranda and Alfred told me—and they're formidable." She leans over to peer in our faces. "Are you brave?"

An odd feeling passes over me, something like an electric chill. I take Lucas's hand and squeeze it. "Yes. We are."

"Then perhaps you could come with me. With your talents you'll be better equipped to get other talented folks to help too."

Lucas seems like he's coming alive again. Having a purpose like this helps.

"We'll do it," I say. "But where do we start?"

Alsa grins. She presses the book into my hands. "This is a history of talented folks which contains the only known records on sky shakers. Look for signs and commonalities. Also, you'll want help from those involved in the network—"

Before she can finish her sentence, someone pounds on her front door. She pales and ushers us into a back room, then presses a hidden button that reveals a sliding panel and small chamber beyond. "Stay here," she says, nudging us inside. Then the panel slides back, and she's gone from view.

On the inside of the chamber are two buttons, one to open and one to close, but we don't dare press either without permission. The shadows deepen around us. Wide-eyed, we sit in the dark room and wait and listen. Dar is still and quiet inside my bag; I hope she understands the importance of remaining silent.

We can't make out words, but we hear the bang of the door being shoved open. Alsa shouts, but it gradually gets softer, as though she's being dragged away. Then more noises—beds and tables being upended, cabinets and drawers emptied, bookshelves tipped over. With every clang and bang our pulses spike.

But no one finds our hiding spot. And Alsa does not return, even when the noises fade and the door to the shop slams shut.

We wait, shivering, for one more hour before we dare to open the panel. Then we venture out into the ransacked house.

CHAPTER SIX

We flee the village and walk all night, cloaked in my shadows, praying that Lady Aisling's hunters are not too close behind. By the time dawn stretches across the sky, we are far from the village and deep in the Abbachon territory. The terrain shifts from rock and sand to the outskirts of old-growth woods. Tall, leafy trees tower over our heads and long, clinging vines brush our shoulders and muss up Lucas's hair. Moss coats the thick tree trunks, and bits of pollen wander through the air, making me sneeze.

The shadows cast by the foliage are dark and deep, and I pull a few with me from the undergrowth as we pass. They swirl around my fingers in greeting. Lucas's parents opted to skirt this forest when we made our way to the ocean cottage, but it will be easier to lose the hunters here than on the road.

When the sun is fully risen, we stop to rest our aching legs and eat. I have some bread and cheese in my satchel, and Lucas has apples and jerky in his. He also has some coins stashed away in the bottom, put there by his parents when we first moved to Abbacho, just in case.

Lucas stretches his legs in front of him and yawns as he hums, toasting a piece of bread for us to split. The edges crisp to a perfect golden brown under his direction. We have been quiet through most of our flight from the village, but there is much to say and decide.

He breaks the bread in half and hands me a piece. His face is drawn and pale, even more so than the previous night, with shadows painting the hollows under his eyes. We must find a place to sleep for a couple hours.

"I'm sorry," I say quietly. Lucas keeps his eyes cast down, toeing a fallen stick with one shoe.

"Me too," he says.

"We'll find your parents. And then we can free that sky shaker too."

He snorts. "How? Trying to save them will mean our own capture. We were supposed to be safe with Alsa and even she got caught." He kicks the stick, and it bounces off a nearby tree.

I swallow the last of my toast, then begin to rifle through my bag. "We need help."

The familiar light of curiosity and hope gleams in Lucas's eyes. "Help from whom?"

"The network, of course." I hold up the scroll from his parents proudly. "Have your parents ever shown you this?"

Lucas frowns and shakes his head.

"It's a list of all the known talented folks born in the last two hundred years." I unravel the scroll, showing him how far back it goes and the names that have been crossed out. "And it has the last known location as well. Which means, if we can find all the talented left who live here in Abbacho before Lady Aisling's men do, we might be able to rally them against her. At the very least, they may be able to point us to whoever leads the network, and then we can hand over the task to them. I'm sure they'd know what to do and the best way to go about freeing your parents."

Lucas's face brightens cautiously. "But this is a big territory. Some of them may be hard to find."

"That's true. But we also have all these files from your parents, remember?" I pull out a couple of the papers they stashed in my bag last night. "I haven't looked at them yet, but if your parents were so keen that Lady Aisling not know the contents, I think it's a safe bet that they will help us."

A smile finally crosses Lucas's face, and it's like the sun rising a second time. "Brilliant," he says. "I bet the Rodans' new location is in here somewhere. We should find them first. They'll help us."

I'm sure they'd be delighted to see Lucas, but not me. The last time I saw them, I inadvertently brought Lady Aisling's men down on our heads, and they were none too happy.

He begins digging through the papers in his bag, and I do the same with mine, starting with the ones on top. The first few are deeds to properties, but the names don't seem to match the ones on the scroll. Puzzled, I set them aside.

A small voice whines from inside my bag. "Emmeline, I'm hungry. It has been hours since I've eaten anything."

I pull out Dar's cage and quickly shove a small chunk of bread and cheese through the bars. She eyes the papers on my lap shrewdly while she chews.

"What are you up to?" she asks.

"Never you mind," I say.

"If it has anything to do with Lady Aisling, let me help." She moves closer to the bars. "Please, I want to help!"

Lucas sighs and turns his back to us.

"No, Dar, we can't trust you yet. You know that. And this has nothing to do with Lady Aisling. If we need your help, we'll ask you, I promise."

"But—"

"I'm sorry, but I think it's time you went back." I return her cage to my bag, but her angry objections still sound in my ears.

Lucas leans against a tree trunk, vines dangling just above his head. He valiantly tries to remain awake to examine the papers, but nods off every few seconds. I put a hand on his arm.

"Rest. I'll take the first watch."

He smiles gratefully and closes his eyes. I do my best to stay alert for any hunters or dangerous animals that may approach. At first, the papers help, but soon the words begin to blur together. Finally I put them away and practice twirling shadows instead to keep me occupied. But before long, sleep falls over me and carries me away.

In my dreams, we are being pursued by Lady Aisling and her men. They chase us over the hills and through the woods. And then they catch us. We are yanked off our feet, my own shadow ropes somehow turned against me as Lady Aisling consumes my power. I can only whimper and wish Dar was here, free to do as she pleased to her evil sister.

As if she can hear my thoughts, Dar begins to scream from my bag a few feet away, startling me awake.

"Emmeline! Emmeline! Where are you? Have you abandoned me?" she screeches. Her muffled sobs echo louder than I would have thought possible.

I snatch up my bag and open it as Lucas begins to wake. "Dar!" I scold. "Be quiet. Or you'll alert every predator in the forest to our presence. And Lady Aisling's men for good measure."

She immediately quiets down to sulk. "How would I know where we are? It's stuffy and I can't see anything in here. You weren't answering, and I thought you'd tired of me at last."

"We can't risk taking you out." I fold my arms over my chest. Arguing with Dar is exhausting.

"You've grown so unkind." Dar huffs and sits at the bottom of her cage with her back to me. I sigh and close my bag.

"Maybe we should make her a shadow-and-light muzzle too," Lucas says.

"I heard that," comes Dar's muffled response from within my bag.

I suppress a smile.

We set out again, more warily this time. We fall into a rhythm as we walk. My mind strays back to the papers we examined earlier. Something about the housing deeds troubles me. Why aren't the names on any of the lists his parents kept? Why would they need those deeds? They do not appear to be old, but recent, within the last few years.

I stop to search through my bag, meeting a grumble or two from Dar, and pull out one of the deeds. Lucas eyes me strangely.

"What are you doing?"

I thrust the papers into his hands. "Look at this." He glances it over and shrugs.

"It's a deed to some property in Abbacho."

"It is, and the names don't match any of the ones on our list of talented people."

He stares at me like I have two heads, and I begin to laugh. "They're aliases. That's why your parents have copies of the deeds. They've been helping talented folks find new homes across the territories. They don't match the real names on the list because these are fake!"

Lucas's face lights up. "So we find these properties and we'll find other talented people who might be able to help us."

"Exactly." I grin, but glance around nervously. "But first we need to get out of this forest."

With a renewed bounce in our steps, we march on, hopeful that we might have found what we need.

⟵ • ⟶

It is midday when Dar begins to rattle her cage again. The whining of her little voice in my satchel is worse than a fly buzzing in my ears. No one else is in sight, so I finally take her out.

I hold up her cage to eye level while Lucas scowls next to me.

"What is it now, Dar?"

"It's about time," she says. "Make my cage bigger, please. I need to get out."

I almost laugh. Does she really believe it will be that easy? "I don't think so."

She puts her tiny hands on her hips. Is it odd that I have almost gotten used to talking to a tiny version of myself?

"Listen to me," Dar says. "I know Lady Aisling. She is my own flesh and blood. And I know Zinnia."

"What does that matter?" Lucas says. "That has nothing to do with whether we can trust you."

Dar's gaze snaps to Lucas. "Do you ever want to see your parents again?" He flinches. "I know how to move around in that territory. I can help you get them back."

Lucas swallows hard, his hands balling into fists. "We're never letting you out. Get used to living in that cage, because you're going to be there for a very long time."

With that, Lucas stomps ahead of me at a faster pace. I can still see him, but I don't try to catch up. Instead I talk to Dar while I follow him.

"You need me," Dar says.

"Well, I have you. You're right here in your cage where you belong."

She narrows her eyes. "You need me to guide you and protect you from Lady Aisling. No one knows her like I do."

I consider Dar for a long moment. On occasion I've tried to broach the subject of her early life with Lady Aisling, but she always changes the subject. "You say you know her, but you've never really told me about what happened between you."

Dar looks away before answering. "My sister should've been closer to me than anyone else. Twins are supposed to share everything, aren't they? But she hated me from the beginning. It was because our parents liked me best. I was nicer, happier, and I had an amusing talent, while she was sickly and sullen and had no magic as far as we could tell. They doted on me, and she never forgave me for it. She punished me for it too." She stamps a foot on the floor of the cage. "Every chance she had she'd play a cruel joke or trick at my expense. The more my parents scolded her, the angrier she got."

I shiver. Lady Aisling played tricks on Dar? That must be where Dar got all her ideas for the games she convinced me to play on others. A tiny crack forms in my heart, joining the others that have appeared each time I've learned more about Dar's past.

She continues, "Then one day, she broke my ankle. My parents threatened to send her away to finishing school. She was more furious than I've ever seen her before. She came into my room late at night after our parents were in bed and put her hands around my neck. That was how she discovered her powers. Her focus on wanting to take what I had so our parents would love her too finally brought her powers to light." She chokes on her words. Tears glimmer in the corner of her—my—eyes just before they flash violently.

"And then she did take it. Everything. All my power, gone." Dar shudders. "When she strangled me, I tried to shift, but I couldn't escape. She only needs to be in close proximity to a person to steal their powers. I could feel it flowing out of me and into her body. I had no idea what was happening, only that I was getting weaker and weaker and that I didn't want to go. I didn't want to die. Since my talent was inherent to my body, it didn't survive, but she could never touch my soul. But everything that had made me *me* was gone, sucked dry. My body crumbled to dust, and I was doomed to wander the shadow worlds, not dead and yet not quite alive, only a glimmer of my former self. I could see life happening, time passing around me, but I couldn't take part. Not until you found me and made me yours."

"That's horrible. I'm sorry, Dar."

Dar's face twists. "Oh, that wasn't all she did. She took my life. Pretended to be me for a time since she had my talent. She basked in our parents' attention, telling them some lie that she had run away, but she could only fool them for so long. Eventually she got bored of shape shifting. She couldn't help herself; she had to devour another talent. When our parents realized she could no longer shape shift, they knew the truth. They shunned her, but their timing was tragic. She had recently stolen the talent from a lightning caller and had no idea how to control it. Her rage brought the lightning down on all of them. Our parents did not survive."

My heart aches in my chest. I have no idea what to say. There is no comfort I can give.

"She may have better control now, but she is just as wicked at heart as she always was." Dar scowls. "Don't go up against her on your own. You will be captured. She will imprison you in her garden. And then what will become of me?"

My breath catches in my throat. I am responsible for Dar, and I don't want her to get caught either. She has already been through enough. "That won't happen. We're going to find more allies first, then we'll go to Zinnia. We don't need you for that. But I do need to keep you out of Lady Aisling's grasp."

"Then you will fail. Do not underestimate her, Emmeline." Dar shakes the bars in frustration, sprouting a couple claws and horns in the process. "For goodness' sake, she changed the path of the Cerelia Comet just so she could have more powers to harvest earlier. She is insatiable!"

Cold prickles over my back, but I shake it off. Dar is trying to get under my skin. I can't let her succeed.

"She won't find us." I put on a brave face, but this scares me more than I'm willing to let Dar know. "If we band together with other talented people, we will be better able to defeat her."

"You are fooling yourself. And it will be the end of us all." Dar sinks to the floor of her cage with her back to me, arms crossed as she sulks.

I return her cage to my satchel, shaking my head. As much as I hate to admit it, there is a part of me that can't help wondering if Dar has a point. She knows more about the trouble we're in than any of us, especially after the loss of Lucas's parents. And she's made it clear she will only help us if we let her out.

But the risks of letting her loose... Well, we know that all too well. Last time, she hurt too many people, she was so bent on revenge. I can't let that happen again.

We shall simply have to find another way. I only hope our plan works.

I pick up the pace, and when I reach Lucas, he is still fuming about what Dar said. His hands clench and unclench and sparks of light spit from his fingertips.

I put a hand on his shoulder. "Don't worry. We'll find your parents. We'll rescue them from Lady Aisling."

"We are not letting Dar go," he says.

"Of course we're not. She's too dangerous. I know that. And I know all her tricks too." I brush a spark from his golden hair. "If you don't calm down, you might set yourself on fire."

Lucas stops for a moment, a laugh bursting from his lips in a way I haven't heard since Lady Aisling came for us. He takes a deep breath and sighs.

"Sorry," he says. "I just really miss them."

"I know," I say. "I do too."

They've been kinder to me than my own parents ever were. And I'm just as determined as Lucas to get them back.

CHAPTER SEVEN

The shadows in the forest are growing darker and deeper—the way I feel safest—when we stop to make camp. Lucas offers to collect some firewood to light with his magic. I am left alone with my thoughts, fears, and hopes.

I toy with the shadows, weaving them into a tent-like structure to lend us shelter. The shadow ropes wrap around two of the nearest trees, and the front opens into flaps to let us slip inside. It wasn't until recently I realized other talented people could feel the shadows I weave. For years I thought it was a secret just between me and Dar.

It's nice to be able to share it now, and I've taught Lucas how to do it with his light singing too.

I sit on a nearby stump, waiting for Lucas to return and playing with the shadows, when I hear Dar.

"I'm hungry, Emmeline," she whines. I pull her out and set her cage on the ground beside me. She looks tiny and fragile, and it adds another crack to my heart.

I may as well feed her now and get it over with before Lucas comes back. That way he won't have to listen to her whining too. I break off a couple pieces of leftover jerky and bread and push it through the bars. She devours them eagerly.

I look away, hoping she'll give me some peace, but my eyes snap back at her violent coughing fit. Dar's face turns red, then as purple as the dress she wears.

"Dar!" I cry.

Her mouth is open but she can't seem to form words. For a fleeting moment I wonder if she might be faking it, but when her lips turn blue and she stumbles to the floor of her cage, I'm sure she's not.

I'm responsible for her, my former best friend. I can't just let her die.

At first, I try to reach a finger through the cage to pat her back and help her dislodge whatever is stuck in her throat, but the cage is too tiny and when I make it bigger, I can no longer reach her. Her face turns more blue, and the coughing grows louder and hoarser. She sprawls on the floor, and then an even worse sound begins—silence.

Terror shoots through my limbs. I open the cage door and pull her out, shaking her in the hope that will dislodge the offending piece of food. She is limp in my hands, her eyes rolling back in her head.

"Dar, please, wake up." I try to remember what people do to help someone who is choking. Something about patting their back or their chest. I try both, and only after I tap her chest a couple times do her eyes flutter open again.

Relief floods through me, but just for a moment. Without warning, Dar leaps out of my hands, a terrible cackle bursting free from her lips as she skitters into a bed of ferns nearby.

"Free! Free, free, free, free!" she sings.

"No! Come back, you must. Please!" Panic courses through my veins, the enormity of my mistake making my legs weak. I crash through the undergrowth, trying to capture her again. I catch a glimpse of Dar as she transforms into a rabbit. I send a shadow net sweeping after her, catching her up. But as I frantically pull her toward me, her front paws shift into claws tearing a hole in my net. She slips through and bounds off again.

I race after her, slowing her down by sending my shadows to grab her again and again.

Dar only laughs, reveling in her newfound freedom. She's toying with me.

Suddenly, I'm flying toward the ground, my foot caught on an exposed root. I tumble into the ferns, and by the time I sit up, I can no longer see Dar.

"Thank you, Emmeline," Dar's voice calls, getting softer by the second. It sounds like she is above me now, and I glance up just in time to see the flash of a white wing flying up, up, up in the canopy. Horror settles on my chest with a sickening weight.

What have I done?

I throw up my shadow ropes, a last-ditch effort to catch her, but she shivers out of them easily, then flies off into the night. I need Lucas's light to work with my shadows in order to contain her. She timed her escape perfectly. Purposely.

Tears prick at my eyes. Dar is loose, and it is all my fault. She is free to wreak whatever havoc she pleases. Any harm she does is on my head. More damage for me to make amends for. It is more than I can bear.

But what was I supposed to do? Risk letting her die? I couldn't do that either. She knows me too well. She knew I'd have to help her.

Once again, Dar used me against myself.

I collapse in the leaves, my head in my hands, letting the tears fall until I hear someone coming through the woods, and the soft whisper of Lucas singing a light to brighten his path in the dark.

How can I tell Lucas? How can I admit what I've done? He will be furious, and disappointed.

Lucas reaches the clearing where we set up camp and calls my name. My heart pounds as I rise to my feet and slowly return to face him. When he sees my grim expression, his smile falters.

"What's wrong, Emmeline?" he asks.

Our small shadow-and-light cage rests forgotten against the tree stump. I swallow the knives in my throat.

"Dar is gone."

The color drains from Lucas's face. "What do you mean gone?"

More tears well in my eyes. "She tricked me," I say with a hoarse whisper. "I thought she was choking. She was turning all sorts of horrible colors. I couldn't let her die; I had to try to save her. And after I did, she leaped out of my grasp and fled." I shake my head. "I tried, but I couldn't catch her. I'm sorry, Lucas. I know better than to trust her."

I sink onto the tree stump now that I've made my confession. I can't even look at him for fear of what he must think of me. The world in front of my eyes swims. A moment later Lucas's warm arms wrap around me in a hug.

"I'm sorry, Emmeline," he says quietly. "She has always been a trickster, while you are honest and true."

I did not think I could cry any harder, but I prove myself wrong. Forgiveness, it turns out, was the most unexpected thing.

CHAPTER EIGHT

I take the first watch, letting Lucas sleep. It feels as though we've been awake forever. Dar's empty cage is back in my satchel, intact, just in case we capture her again. Until then, we shall be watching our backs.

It is hard to believe she is really gone, my once constant companion. Despite everything she did, I can't help but miss her presence.

As Lucas drifts off in the shadowcrafted bedroll, I settle into my perch on a rock, pulling the forest's shadows around me like armor. The deep woods are lively at night, full of predatory rumbles, hisses, and rustling. Above me, the moon glows through the occasional break in the canopy, along with a twinkling star or two. Out here alone in a strange place, the world feels far more vast than I ever realized. I've come a long way from the sheltered girl who never left her parents' mansion. I had no idea my world was so small. It revolved around Dar and my magic, and nothing else mattered to me. Ironically, that is why I left in the first place—to keep the things most precious to me safe.

But now I've seen more, learned more, and understand more. The world is bigger than me and my small worries, my single talent. And there are threats out there that would harm this world, like Lady Aisling and Dar. They must be stopped. Somehow. I may not know much, but I know I must do my part to make a difference. My actions no longer affect only me, they ripple outward over many others.

I pull out the book that Alsa gave us and crack it open, hoping to find something useful inside. To my surprise, there is more on magic eaters than just Lady Aisling, though she is certainly the most creative.

A magic eater must exercise their talent regularly, feeding on talents and their effects in order to survive. Without a steady supply they will grow sickly and may even die. This naturally poses a problem for other talented people, making magic eaters one of the most feared of all talents. Fortunately, they are also among the rarest, with only three documented cases in the last five hundred years...

My heart races as I read about the other magic eaters, but sadly the book does not provide ideas on how to stop them. It seems to suggest letting them devour the fruits of your talent and going on your way as quickly as possible. Disappointed, I read on about several other talents such as dream eaters, rain dancers, storm brewers, talent takers, memory stealers, mind readers, and many more. But my thoughts keep returning to magic eaters. Lady Aisling isn't going to willingly stop eating magic. She can't. Reasoning with her, pleading, even bribing will have no success.

Nonetheless, Lucas and I will have to try to stop her. It seems hopeless, and right now, with Dar on the loose, I'm feeling more desperate than ever. Because Dar was right about one thing: we need her. No one knows Lady Aisling like she does. Dar was our secret weapon.

I curl my legs up to my chest and wrap my arms around my knees.

And now she's gone.

←——•——→

When the next morning greets us, we pack up our things and press on. We're not completely certain which deed belongs to the Rodans, but Lucas found one with a name that he believes he heard them mention before. We've decided to head in that direction and to try any network houses in our path along the way.

While I was on watch, I reviewed more of the papers from Lucas's parents and identified several houses that will be on our route. One of the deeds I discovered was for a property in what appears to be this very forest. Every deed has a little map along with it, and as far as I can tell this one points to somewhere in this mess of ancient trees and vines.

We walk as quickly as we can, using the mountains that peek through the trees to orient ourselves on the map. We know better than to stay in one place for long. We make good time despite the clinging vines, hanging branches, and shrubbery so thick that only one of Miranda's largest, sharpest knives could cut through it.

At last we reach an area deep in the woods full of trees with trunks wider than a horse is long and branches that extend in all directions. Their shadows loom over us. Thick green vines drape over everything, and the forest floor is littered with blooming flowers. This is where the map led us. We glance around, hoping for a hint as to where this home is supposed to be.

Lucas frowns at the drawing of the map. He turns it around several times. "Maybe we're in the wrong place?"

I shake my head. "No, this is definitely it. See?" I indicate the mountain range on the map. "The mountains are that way. And we came from this way." I point to the south and the ocean.

"Well, then where is it?"

I shrug. "It's got to be here somewhere."

The sun is high overhead, but Lucas illuminates the shadowed nooks and crannies. I examine each one, carefully searching for a hint of something out of place, something that resembles an entrance to a house. We retreat to the center of the giant tree grove, still puzzled as ever.

Then the laughter begins.

It comes from somewhere over our heads, and we glance up. Lucas snuffs out his light. At first, we can't tell exactly where it comes from, then it gets louder and more raucous.

"Who are you?" I yell in frustration.

A new noise rings out, one of gears and a hissing that makes my skin crawl. Something whooshes over us, and we duck down in surprise.

We quickly get to our feet and find a little girl with a round cherubic face giggling behind us. She cannot be more than seven years old, and she's dressed in simple clothing that provides excellent camouflage both from predators and from Lady Aisling's hunters, no doubt. A little bit of dirt is smudged across her nose and cheeks, though it's hard to tell whether that's an accident or intentional. She holds a rope knotted at the end, which she used to swing down to the ground.

She is very amused at our confusion.

"Who are you?" she asks when she finally stops laughing.

"I'm Lucas, and this is Emmeline. What's your name?" Lucas says. The sudden appearance of this little girl makes me want to throw up my shadows and hide. But we've traveled too far to stop now.

"I'm Cheyenne," the girl says, absentmindedly putting one dirty thumb in her mouth. I cringe.

"Does your family live around here?" I ask.

Cheyenne grins. "We live up there." She points up into the nearest giant tree. Could these trees all be homes?

"Are you going to stay with us?" she blurts out, the hope in her voice mirrored by the hope on her face. We expected to encounter people whose trust we'd have to work hard to earn; this girl is much too welcoming. She knows nothing about us. She's very young, but I can't shake the feeling that something isn't right.

"Maybe just for a night, if that's all right with your parents," Lucas says. "Are they home?"

Cheyenne darts off toward the trunk of the nearest giant tree. "Come on, I'll introduce you!" Her short pigtails flap behind her. She's too young to have been blessed by the comet, but if she has an older sibling who is talented, I'd hate to see her be so forward with Lady Aisling and her men.

She leads us around to the back of the tree. Several more ropes hang down to the forest floor hidden among the vines. She steps between them and gestures for us to do the same. Then she yanks on a rope that hangs in the middle, and suddenly we are moving up, up, up on a wooden platform.

I gasp. The girl has no trouble, but I hold on to Lucas to keep my balance. He seems just as surprised as I am. We rise through the foliage, huge green leaves bigger than my entire body brushing by us as we pass. Birds flutter off, seeking a calmer spot in the canopy. Everything is green, spotted with alternating bands of shadow and light.

When the contraption finally stops, we're in for another surprise. Cheyenne ties the rope to a branch, securing the platform to a deck that rests high up in the trees. Just beyond it is a door attached to an expansive hut that spreads throughout the giant tree's branch network. It is far larger than the cottages I've become accustomed to, though not quite as large as the mansion I once called home.

Lucas's eyes bulge. "This place is enormous! How many people are in your family?"

Cheyenne laughs again. "Just me and my parents. And my sister, but she's away right now."

Lucas and I exchange a quick look. She does have a sister, and that sibling must be the talented one. Though it seems strange for her to be away, especially with Lady Aisling's hunters on the move.

"Just the four of you?" I say.

She shrugs. "Well, we do have guests from time to time. I love guests." She grins widely, and my heart sinks. This poor girl would greet those hunters just as warmly as us, I have no doubt. "Come on," she says, opening the door.

The interior is cleverly crafted. Everything is made from trees and leaves and woven branches, with an eye to blend and conceal. A perfect place for members of the network wanting to keep their talented children safe. We'd never have found this without Cheyenne's help. She takes us across the cavernous front room into a smaller area in the back, almost like a study. A man sits at a desk. He has his back to us, but he looks up when he hears our shoes on the floor.

He's older and nothing like Alfred or my own father. His clothes are simple and rugged like the girl's, his face is weather-worn, and his hair is shorn close to his scalp. I wonder for a moment if he built this massive tree house himself and hope he isn't angry that we stand here without an invitation. My hands wring together involuntarily.

But the surprise lifts from his face, and he smiles broadly. Fear and suspicion of strangers seems a foreign thing to this family.

"Cheyenne," he says, "who did you bring home today?"

She laughs. "Emmeline and Lucas. They wanted to talk to you and Mum."

He holds out a hand to us. "I'm Galen. My wife, Tali, is somewhere around here. Welcome to our home."

Lucas and I shake his hand in a daze as a tall woman with long dark hair and green eyes enters the room. She too, smiles.

"I thought I heard voices," she says.

"Cheyenne brought home some more stragglers. This is Emmeline and Lucas," Galen says.

"You are welcome here," Tali says.

"So," Galen sits back and gestures to a long bench carved from the wall of the study. "What brings you to our grove?"

Lucas speaks first. "You, I think. Unless you happen to have neighbors."

Tali laughs. "No, it is just us. No one else lives near here for miles."

"We're searching for people with talents. We thought perhaps one might live here?" I say.

Cheyenne brightens up. "Yes! Nova has a talent."

"But it isn't a very useful one, and I'm afraid you've come all this way for nothing," Galen says. "She's not here, and we do not expect her to return for some time."

"Where is she?" I ask, hoping I am not trying their patience and kindness too much.

"The most wonderful place," Tali says wistfully, resting a hand on her husband's shoulder. "She was recruited for a special school where she's trained along with other talented children. She is happy there and writes to us every week."

Galen pats his wife's hand. "We are very proud of her." Something about their eyes, a faraway look, strikes me as odd.

A knot forms in the pit of my stomach, growing more uncomfortable with every breath. "She was recruited? By whom? How long ago?" I know full well no such school exists.

"A kindly, rich woman seeking talented children came here ages ago. Cheyenne found her and her serving boy outside in the grove and brought them home." Galen tugs on one of Cheyenne's pigtails and laughs. "Lovely woman. She saw so much potential in Nova that she offered to sponsor our daughter herself that same evening. Of course, we could not let such an extraordinary opportunity pass."

"We miss her, of course," Tali says, "but we know it is for the best and that she is very happy."

"Yes, it is for the best," Galen echoes.

I am frozen to the seat. Lucas's face contorts. Lady Aisling was here—no longer leaving the recruiting just to her henchman apparently. She must have spelled them with one of her many stolen talents. Something that made them believe her, removed their suspicion, even though they should have known better if they were part of the network. People didn't just move to such remote places for fun.

They do it to hide their children from *her*.

"Would you like to join us for dinner?" Tali asks. "You are welcome to spend the night before you continue on your way."

"Thank you," Lucas says. "We'd appreciate that."

While his words are warm, his eyes betray his fears. He must be thinking the same thing I am.

Something terrible has happened to Nova. We've arrived too late.

CHAPTER NINE

Later that evening when the house has gone to sleep, I creep from the room Tali and Galen gave me for the evening. They have many rooms here. Many empty rooms. Almost like this place was meant to house far more people—maybe even created as a resting point for travelers hoping to escape Lady Aisling's clutches.

And now it has fallen into her grasp.

I wrap my shadows around me, weaving them into a giant cloak, then sneak across the hall to Lucas's room. I knock once, just loud enough for him to hear, then slip inside. When the door closes behind me, I release the shadows. Lucas yawns and sits up in his bed, rubbing his eyes. I perch on the edge, every muscle in my body tense with the fear of being discovered.

"We need to talk," I say. Lucas blinks more of the sleep from his eyes.

"I know. Something is not at all right here. They didn't even question why we're wandering the woods alone. I thought for certain we'd need to give them some excuse."

"We shouldn't let them see that we have talents like their daughter." I shiver. "If Lady Aisling was here, she may have a means of watching. It's too risky."

Lucas nods his agreement. "They're far too calm about sending their daughter off with a strange woman for people involved with the network."

My heart plunges into my toes as a horrible thought grabs me. "We may need to consider the possibility that the network has been compromised. That Lady Aisling has infiltrated it."

"That would explain how Alsa got caught." Lucas is quiet for a moment. "Should we stop seeking help?"

"Definitely not. It's also possible we're too suspicious." I give a wry laugh. "That's why we need to find out. I'm going to sneak into their study to search for any clues about Nova or the network."

Lucas swings his feet off the bed. "I'm coming with you."

I form a shadow cocoon around us both, then we tiptoe out into the hall. Having Lucas with me is comforting, almost like having Dar here, back when I thought she was my best friend.

No one wakes as we make our way to the study; only soft snores echo through the master bedroom doors. I breathe out in relief, but I keep up my guard. Lucas's eyes are wide as though every shadow could be Lady Aisling or her hunters. Lucky for me, I know shadows when I see one, and nothing can hide in them from me.

When we reach the study, we sneak inside and rummage through every drawer we can find as quickly and quietly as possible.

"Here!" I hiss when my hands alight on an envelope with a broken seal deep in one of the bottom drawers. Lucas draws near, and we read it silently together.

Dear Mama and Pa,

Zinnia is the most beautiful place. The Lady was right; the school is perfect for me, and I am making many friends.

Thank you for sending me. I am so
happy here! I cannot wait to show you
all I have learned when I come home.

Love,

Nova

The letter is short and sweet, and Nova does sound happy. Could we be wrong? Could there be some other woman who is offering to train children who are talented? It seems very unlikely, but I suppose we cannot yet rule it out. Still, there is something about the letter that unsettles me. I am anxious to be rid of it. I stuff it back in the drawer where it belongs.

"That didn't offer us much information, did it?" Lucas whispers.

I shake my head. "I'd hoped for more. I think it best we leave here as early as possible in the morning. Just to be safe."

"Agreed."

Together we sneak back into the hallway, but as we pass a window that looks out at the night sky, Lucas touches my arm. The moon is nearly full and bright, and the stars glitter. But something else moves in the sky. A cluster of objects—smaller than stars—bursts apart and falls from the heavens to the earth. I swallow hard, remembering what Alsa said about how moving the comet might upset other things in the heavens.

"Do you think those were meteors?" whispers Lucas.

"Maybe."

We make our way back to our rooms, our hearts and minds troubled. When I sink into my guest bed, I stare at the ceiling for a long while, tossing and turning. As I do, a slip of paper falls from underneath my pillow to the floor. Curious, I retrieve it.

The Lady watches this house.
Leave at first light, or she'll
come for you too.

A chill spreads over my entire body. Who left this note? Nova? Some other traveler? I tuck it back under the pillow. It's a warning others should heed too if this is meant to be some sort of way station for the network.

Eventually I fall into a slumber filled with dreams of a dark, dangerous woman lurking in the shadows while the heavens crash to the earth all around us.

CHAPTER TEN

The next morning we set out at dawn after thanking our hosts for their hospitality and the extra provisions they've given us for the road and bidding them a hasty goodbye. We do not wish to remain there any longer than necessary.

We spend the day hurrying through the woods. Everywhere I look are signs of other people now—broken branches and pits that might have once held a fire—where before the forest had seemed wild and untraveled. We may not be as alone as we'd thought.

By midafternoon we've left the old-growth section behind, the terrain changing to a sparse, mountainous forest similar to the one we left by the seashore. We travel as far as we can, but it is near midnight when we have to admit we will not reach the village where the next home on our list is before morning. The moon shines high above us, and the stars light our way, but our feet are worn out and we must rest. Thankfully, no meteors light up the sky tonight. Maybe Alsa's warnings were just cautionary and not prophetic.

"We should go back to that quarry we passed a little while ago," I suggest. "It would provide better shelter than anything out here."

The forest is thinner, which makes me feel exposed. We're nearing an area that marks the border between Abbacho and Parilla. I can set my shadows up anywhere, but we still need cover to remain undiscovered by other travelers in the night. The quarry would be perfect.

"Good idea," Lucas says, and we head back over the hill we just passed. The quarry is a huge swath of land, the white stone cut in angles making it seem as though it was crafted into steps for giants long ago. We find a spot where the steps are not as sharp and far between and clamber down to the bottom. We do need to come back up in the morning, after all.

We choose a spot near the wall to set up camp. I craft

a shadow tent that will prevent anyone glancing down from spying us. Then I form two sleeping rolls with plush shadow pillows. Lucas collapses onto one of them. "Someday I'll be able to make something this big and control it like you do," he says.

I lay across from him on the other bedroll. "I just wish we had better luck finding other talented folks." I shudder.

"We'll get my parents back, and then we'll find a way to get the others who've been taken back too," Lucas says. "We have to."

I wish I felt as confident as he sounds. Ever since we left the tree house this morning, fear has nipped at my heels, following me everywhere as if it were a replacement for my lost shadow.

Lucas's soft snores mix with the night songs of owls and insects and howling animals in the distance. Through the shadow tent, the sky twinkles as though nothing at all has changed. The same stars still shine, and the moon begins its nightly trek across the sky. You'd never know that only a few nights ago, the Cerelia Comet left its normal path to fly over our territories too early. Unlike last night's display, the heavens give no sign anything has changed.

And yet, everything has.

Dar is on the loose, Lady Aisling is in Abbacho hunting us, and Lucas and I are on our own until we can find more people involved in the network. I wrap a shadow blanket around me and shiver.

I try to sleep, but end up staring at the sky above, watching the stars twinkle through my shadows for far longer than usual.

Suddenly I sit straight up in my bedroll.

I'd swear I just heard the sound of horses braying and horseshoes clattering over rocks. It comes again, unmistakable this time. Something cold wraps around my shoulders and slithers down my back. Even though we're hidden in the shadow tent, I gather more shadows and cloak myself in them.

One can never be too careful.

The hoofbeats are getting closer, and there is little chance I will sleep now. I must know if it is the hunters. If it *is* the hunters, we need to be prepared. I swallow the biting fear, and sneak out of the tent, careful not to wake Lucas. It's better if I do this alone. Less risk of being caught.

With my shadows coiled around me, I make my way toward the top of the quarry, warily listening for any snippets of conversations to reach my ears. When I arrive at the top step, I slip into a nook beside it and peek over the edge.

There are horses aplenty and guards too—each garbed in the telltale green cloak of Lady Aisling's men. They appear to be setting up camp. It is close, but we should still be safe all the way at the bottom of the quarry. I hope so, because we have no choice but to wait until they're gone. My heart thumps so loud I fear it will give me away. A word or two reaches my ears, but nothing interesting until I hear "talent taker" between a couple of the guards brushing down their horses for the night.

"Only thing I've ever seen that seemed to trouble the Lady," the first guard says. "But who knows if the rumors are true?"

A talent taker. Someone who can make magic go away, if I remember correctly from what I read in Alsa's history book. I can see why their existence might terrify Lady Aisling. I confess, I find it a little scary myself.

"I doubt it. I bet we're here on a fool's errand, while the Lady is off hunting the girl and boy we've been tracking. That man was desperate. He would have said anything to save his skin. I've never heard of such a thing." The second guard ducks as his horse's tail swishes near his face.

"Still, we can't leave any stone unturned, or it will be our heads on the line instead of the talent taker's."

The second guard grunts as they finish up their task. They're hunting a talent taker. It sounds like Lady Aisling wants to get rid of them. Or perhaps that's the ruse she uses to cover her true purpose? The power to remove magic would be a mighty one indeed. But if Lady Aisling is already gobbling up all the power she can get her hands on, what use would that particular talent be to her?

Puzzled, I poke my head up again once they're gone and search for any other clues. The camp is largely settled now: tents pitched, horses rubbed down, and fires lit. The darkness is held at bay by the firelight, but it would lend more shadows for me to hide between if I felt brave enough to get closer to one of the campfires…

Before I can finish that thought, a flash of white weaving through the camp stops me cold.

Simone.

The strange, unsettling girl I met months ago wanders erratically between the tents, humming to herself. I duck and scramble back down into the quarry.

Under no circumstances can she see me.

She's a mind reader and can sense me even through my shadows. The only stroke of luck is she has no reason to suspect we're here. I move silently down the large steps, keeping to nooks when I can. Anything to remain out of her view. I pray she does not glance into the quarry.

But even if she did, would she bring the hunters running? Or would she let us be? She does not hunt by choice, and when I last saw her it was clear she did what she did only when she was under Lady Aisling's control. My thoughts circle and scatter as I reach the bottom and run to our shadow tent. It is around a corner, keeping it out of her line of sight. I settle into my bedroll once again. I'm terrified to stay here, but even more scared to risk escape. There is only one way out: through the side of the quarry where the hunters made camp.

Lucas sleeps blissfully unaware. I won't wake him unless danger approaches.

I lay back, heart in my throat, wishing in vain for sleep to take me until the sun rises again.

CHAPTER ELEVEN

The sun wakes Lucas before I do. He yawns and stretches, and I kneel next to him with a finger to my lips, causing the smile on his face to falter.

"Emmeline, what—"

"Shh," I whisper. "There is a camp of hunters on the ridge."

Lucas's skin pales.

"They arrived after you fell asleep. They haven't noticed us, but we'll need to wait until they're gone to leave the tent safely."

"Anything good for breakfast?" He tilts his head hopefully at our bags.

"Some bread and apples, mostly." I hand one of the bags to him. He retrieves an apple and begins polishing it on his shirt.

"I suppose we shouldn't use our talents until they're gone either." He looks wistfully at the bread.

"That would be safest." My talent may hide us, but his would give us away.

He leaves the bread in the bag and sticks with the apple. "What do you think they're doing here?"

I shiver, once again remembering Simone. "They're hunting for someone with a talent. I snuck up to the edge of the quarry to spy on them while you were sleeping."

"What kind of talent? Do you know?"

"A couple of the guards said something about a talent taker. It sounded like Lady Aisling is frightened by the possibility of that talent and wants to get rid of them."

Lucas sits up straighter as he finishes his apple. "A talent taker? I've never heard of that one."

I raise my eyebrows. "That's the same thing the guards said. One of them thought they'd been sent on a fool's errand, but the other seemed to believe there was truth to it. I found a reference to one in Alsa's history book too. I'm not keen on running into someone with a talent like that."

"Me neither. I'd hate to lose my magic. It's who I am, you know what I mean?"

"Exactly. I don't know who I'd be without it." It was the

reason I ran away from home in the first place, though that feels so long ago now.

"And I don't want to find out," Lucas adds.

I stand up to check on the hunters' progress packing up camp. Some of them ready their horses, and coils of smoke curl up from fires recently extinguished. But for the time being, the hunters remain seated right atop our only escape route.

"Simone is here too," I say quietly. I've told Lucas and his family the entire story of my flight from my parents' mansion, everything from Dar to Simone to Lady Aisling. And he knows about my encounter with her in the woods the night I made Dar flesh again. He understands exactly what that means.

"Did she see you?" he asks, nervously picking at the apple core.

"No. I saw her wandering through the camp, and I came right back here. If she *had* seen me, I think the hunters would have captured us by now."

"What do you think she's doing with them?"

I shrug, toying with a thread on the edge of my sleeve. "Probably something similar to what she did with Lord Tate—uncovering talented children. With her power, she's uniquely qualified to do it. She knows what people are hiding."

Lucas shivers. "That's creepy."

"And exactly why we need to stay far away from her."

Shouts ring out over the quarry, causing my heart to leap into my throat. But one look confirms that they are beginning to leave. Finally.

"What was that?" Lucas asks.

"They're about to leave. We should be able to go soon."

We pack up our things, and I disperse all my shadows except the ones making up the tent to keep us hidden from prying eyes. Then we wait.

After what feels like forever, the last of the hunters leave. I've seen no hint of Simone since this morning but neither have I risked getting closer to take a real look. From where we hide it seems all is well and clear.

I let my shadows go with a soft word of thanks for protecting us. We take our time trekking to the top of the quarry, in no rush to catch up to the hunters if they happen to be headed in the same direction we are. The sun rises higher, and Lucas comes alive too. He has more energy now and takes the lead, though he's still not as chatty as he was before his parents were captured. I can tell he never stops worrying about them for more than a few minutes. I wonder if my own parents have been worried about me since I left them so many months ago.

We approach the ridge, remaining quiet just in case. I conceal Lucas in a nook with my shadows while I poke my head over the top. I don't see anyone in the clearing or waiting between the sparse trees. Just the smoking remains of campfires.

Despite that, I can't help feeling like eyes are fixed on me. A presence hidden just out of sight.

But I'm just being overly cautious. It has been a strange and dangerous few days.

"It's all right," I whisper to Lucas, and he leaves the safety of my shadows. Together we step out into the open at the top of the quarry.

That feeling of exposure needles into me again, but I push it down. The hunters appear to have gone north, and according to the little map, our next destination is to the east, which is a relief. We move quickly, eager to put as much distance between us and them as possible.

But we haven't gone far when that feeling of being watched gets worse. This time it's accompanied by a rustling. Lucas and I don't say a word for fear of being heard. Up ahead is one of the few older trees, and we duck behind it. We remain there, hearts pounding in our chests, hands squeezed together behind the tree for a full five minutes. No other sounds present themselves.

Lucas lets out a small laugh.

"Probably just a squirrel," he says.

"Probably," I agree.

Finally, when our pulses have returned to normal, we move out from behind the tree.

But we don't get far.

A burst of giggling shoots fear up and down my spine. With a knot in my stomach I wheel around.

"I know you."

Simone stands about twenty feet away near a small pony. Her gauzy, yellowed dress is caked with dirt on the bottom from all the travel, and her eyes have a wilder expression than usual: the toll of Lady Aisling controlling one's mind.

She twirls toward us, singing her constant refrain of "I know you" interspersed with wild laughter. She seems more unhinged than ever.

"Simone," I say. "We're going to leave here, and you will

not follow us." Beside me, Lucas hums, readying his lightcraft to defend ourselves. My shadows are already coiling around my fingertips.

"I know you," she says one last time, then stops a few feet away. "And so does she."

My shadow bands sweep her up and pin her to a tree like shackles, then tether her pony to the tree too. She struggles for a moment, and then begins to laugh again.

Lucas sends his light next, crafting it into a brilliant wall that circles the tree she's shadow-shackled to. It's blinding enough that she won't be able to see us leave through it. Unfortunately, she now has an idea as to the direction we are heading.

But all she does is laugh in that unnerving manner. We can't get away from her fast enough.

I motion to Lucas to follow me to the south. We can travel that way for a bit, then circle around to the village we wish to visit. If they follow us, hopefully they will have already passed by the time we arrive.

"You weren't lying," Lucas says, once we're out of earshot. "She is the creepiest thing I've ever seen."

"I pity her more than anything. She doesn't hunt

voluntarily. It's all Lady Aisling. The last time we met, she warned me of it just before the Lady took over."

"But how does Lady Aisling do it?" Lucas frowns.

"I think it has something to do with what Dar told me about how her magic-eating power sometimes goes wrong, and the subjects become empty shells instead of flowers as she intended. I never really thought about what happened to them after that, but she must use them in other ways. Like Simone."

"You mean there's more out there like her?" Lucas shudders. "Well, you're right about one thing. That girl feels empty. Like there's no light in her at all. No spark. Just nothing."

We walk quickly and quietly, doing our best to leave Simone and our unsettling thoughts far behind us.

CHAPTER TWELVE

W e reach the next village by midmorning. It's a sleepy place, surrounded by tall willow trees with long drooping branches that shelter the town. The houses are all made of the same white stone from the quarry where we stayed last night, with red-thatched roofs and round windows. After finding the local grocer to restock on food supplies, we wander the streets, looking for the street name and number noted on the network's deed.

It's a quiet morning, dotted by birdsong and the occasional chatter of villagers passing by. The shadows here are soft and simple and reach out to me as we walk. But I cannot stop and play with them today. I am so engrossed in the search it takes a moment before I realize something is not right.

Every one of the people we pass gives us a wary glance and moves to the other side of the street. I nudge Lucas.

"Have you noticed that people are avoiding us?"

He shrugs. "Maybe they don't like strangers."

I bite my lip but resist the urge to throw up my shadows to hide. "I suppose you must be right."

But despite Lucas's reassurances, I cannot shake the feeling of angry eyes following me everywhere I go. The strange looks soon combine with hushed whispers. My skin itches, and all I want to do is vanish.

Then, without warning, an elderly woman with a flower cart rushes over, yelling and waving her arms.

"How dare you show your face here again!" I shrink back as she points her finger at my nose. "You're not welcome here, girly."

I am too shocked to speak. Luckily, Lucas jumps in.

"What do you mean 'again'? We've never been here before."

The woman narrows her dark eyes. "I don't know who you are, my boy, but this girl was here just a couple days ago. Running through town like the devil was on her tail, wailing something awful about the comet that passed by a few days ago." The woman straightens up and crosses her arms over her chest. "She knocked over my cart and ruined a whole day's worth of deliveries." She makes a sweeping gesture to the buildings behind her. "Ask anyone here. Everyone saw her raising a ruckus."

"That's impossible," Lucas says. "We've been traveling from the coast. Yesterday we were deep in the forest and made camp near the quarry last night. It wasn't Emmeline."

My heart sinks. "But I do know who it was. Her name is Dar. She's a shape shifter. She likes to take my form."

The old woman considers this. "Well, I suppose that explains how she managed to sprout horns and gave the magistrate a fright when he tried to have her thrown out of town. But how do we know you're not the shape shifter?"

I swallow hard. We have been careful not to let on about our talents, but with the people gathering around us and the weight of their pulsing rage, I don't think I have a choice.

"Because I have a talent already, and it's not shape shifting, it's shadow weaving."

Lucas, though surprised by my admission, doesn't miss a beat. "And no one can have more than one talent."

The woman harrumphs. "Prove it, and we'll let you pass unhindered."

Lucas gives me an encouraging nudge, and I take a deep breath. Then I command the old woman's shadow to twist and wiggle. The woman next to her gasps, and the old lady finally notices. She barks a laugh and breaks into a smile.

"Point taken, my dears. You may pass through. But be quick about your business."

Relief bubbles through me as the villagers disperse, but the woman's warning to be quick resonates. We should not linger here for long. Especially now that they know my talent. It is only a matter of time until Lady Aisling is on our trail once again. We pick up the pace.

"What do you think Dar is up to, coming here?" Lucas asks, frowning thoughtfully.

"It can't be a coincidence she's following the same route we are."

"But how would she know where to go? It doesn't make sense."

I toy with a shadow from the nearby trees, wondering the same thing. Then suddenly I groan. "She was in my bag.

She may have glimpsed the list or seen the deeds." My stomach tightens. "I hope she doesn't scare anyone else off before we can get to them."

"Whatever she's up to, we do know one thing," Lucas says.

"What?"

"That it isn't anything good."

I shiver. He's right, and that concerns me more than I want to admit.

Soon we find the right street and stand in front of the stone and red-thatched roof house that should hold the family with a talented child near our age.

We knock on the front door, but no one answers.

"Perhaps they're not home?" Lucas suggests, but something feels wrong. I step back onto the walkway and examine the house. The windows are dirty, and weeds crowd the small garden running alongside the outside. And the roof—there's a dark spot with singed edges I can't see fully, but I'm willing to bet it's a hole.

My stomach drops into my feet. We're too late. Again.

"Lucas, I don't think they're here. Not anymore."

He frowns. "Let's find out." He tries the doorknob, and

the door creaks open without resistance. We exchange a wary look and step inside. The dim light reveals a small kitchen with a round table surrounded by three empty chairs. A black bowl rests in the center of the table, and upon closer inspection reveals it's actually burned and full of charred fruit. Without a doubt, the talented person who lived here was a fire breather.

"Hello?" Lucas calls, but no one answers. Only dust motes float through the beams of light streaming in from the windows.

We search the house and find no one. When I reach the second bedroom, I halt in the doorway. This must be the fire breather's room. And it must be where they were taken. Everything is black and charred, as though they put up the biggest fight of their life. Maybe this house is empty because they escaped. One can always hope.

Lucas gasps behind me. "Do you think they made it out alive?"

I shrug helplessly. "I hope so." But even I have to admit it doesn't seem promising. I close the door, unable to bear the sight of the room anymore.

Lucas sinks into one of the kitchen chairs, and as he does, a slip of paper floats to the floor. I pick it up. The script is old fashioned but legible enough.

*Beware the hollow dolls. They
are everywhere.*

An odd chill settles over my shoulders. The writing looks the same as the note I found in the tree house. But what are hollow dolls?

"What's that?" Lucas asks, and I show him. He frowns, looking around warily.

I study it for a moment then tuck the paper into my bag for safekeeping.

"What do we do now?" Lucas puts his head in his hands, running his fingers through his hair. The light toys with it—he may have more control over his powers, but he still does things unconsciously.

I pull out the list but don't join him at the table. That charred bowl of fruit is too eerie. Suddenly, my face brightens.

"There's only a couple more homes in Abbacho. One of them must be the Rodans. They've known your family for years. Surely they'll be able to help us form a plan to get your parents back."

Lucas cracks a smile. "It would be nice to see Doyle and Cary again."

"Then let's get going, though perhaps a little more cautiously this time." Now that the villagers know what I can do, I don't want to run into them again. Lady Aisling has spies everywhere. They don't need to know what direction we've gone.

I collect all the shadows in the little house and craft a cloak to cover me and Lucas. Then we sneak away, hoping no one notices the wayward shadow slinking along the edges of the village.

CHAPTER THIRTEEN

The next day, we reach the area where we hope the Rodans' new home is. Lucas remembered Doyle once saying something about them moving close to the border of Parilla, and this fits that description. But we see no sign of a house. The terrain is hilly, with giant boulders sticking out of the earth, like the tips of buried fingers grasping toward the sky. A few scattered trees provide some shade, and a stream snakes between the rocks, the water tumbling over smaller ones and smoothing them.

"Do you think your parents had the right location? Maybe they moved," I say, but Lucas shakes his head.

"No, they would have told my parents. They were close."

"Then where are they?" I throw my hands up.

"They're here somewhere. We'll just have to keep looking."

I scramble on top of the nearest boulder to get a better view of what's nearby. In the distance, the forest sways in the wind. To the other side, and much closer, a cliff rises above the foothills where we search.

Where the terrain evens out into rolling fields in the distance, far to the north beyond the forest and cliff, there is the hint of village rooftops shining in the sun. But not here. The one thing I don't see in these foothills is a house.

I call down to Lucas with my report, and his brow furrows too. But only for a moment. Then his face brightens, glowing with sunshine.

"What is it?" I ask.

"I think I know where they are."

Curious, I drop to the ground. Lucas is already running ahead. The shadows of the boulders trail behind me as I chase after him. They skitter along the ground like fish racing underwater. I am breathless and laughing by the time I reach him.

"Where are they?" I ask, but he only smiles with a spark in his eye.

He leads me toward the cliff, and I can't help wondering what I missed that seems clear to him. The rocks thin out the closer we get, and the stream cuts across to meander a few feet away from the base.

Lucas stops when we reach the cliff face. "My parents once told me about clever homes some in the network create, like the tree house we found. Some are buried in the earth under a hill, burrowed from the trunk of an ancient oak tree, or even carved into a cave. I'm willing to bet their house is built right into this cliff." He frowns. "Somewhere."

I take in the long stretch of rock face we'll need to explore. "That may take a while. You go left, I'll go right. And if we find it, send up sparks or I'll send up a shadow kite. If there's danger, meet back here where the stream runs into the rocks."

Lucas agrees, and we each head in opposite directions. The cliff rises next to me, stretching into the sky and blocking my view of the sun. Now that I'm alone, I swirl the shadow cast by the cliff around my body like a second skin. If any of Lady Aisling's men are nearby, they will not see me. I only hope Lucas is as careful on his side too.

As hopeful as I am we'll have success this time, I'm nervous.

The last time I saw the Rodans was the night Lady Aisling's men found Lucas's family's cottage while they were visiting. They left us, furious. I don't expect a friendly greeting. But I try to put these worries aside and examine the rock wall carefully as I walk, searching for any seam or hint of an entrance. Halfway to the end of the cliff, I hear a shout and sparks shoot up from Lucas's side.

He found something.

I run back toward him, excitement racing through my limbs. I can't help wondering how the Rodans' home is hidden and how far into the rock it goes. The cliff looks big enough to house a palace.

I release my shadows when I reach Lucas. "What did you find?"

"Here," he says, pointing to a perfectly straight seam in the rock—too straight to be natural. My eyes follow it up where it meets a second seam, this one horizontal, that stretches until it hits yet another vertical seam that goes back into the ground.

The outline of a door. One I'd never have noticed if we hadn't been looking for it.

I grin. "Should we knock?"

"Definitely."

Together we each hold up a hand to the rock and rap soundly three times. It echoes, like something vast and unknown hides behind it. Scarcely daring to breathe, we wait for an answer. It feels like an eternity passes before anything happens.

But then something creaks and clicks, and the outline of the door begins to sink into the cliff face. It swings open, revealing a girl a little older than us standing in the doorway—Cary. Shock lines her face, then she lets out a small cry and rushes forward to throw her arms around us both.

Finally, we have found someone we had hoped to find.

But before relief can fully wash over us, it's clear something isn't right. Cary is crying—not a thing I'd ever have expected from her. She didn't cry even when Lady Aisling's men had Lucas's old cottage surrounded.

She pulls back, her face red and puffy. "I'm glad you're here." She wipes her eyes. "Where are your parents? Maybe they can help us."

All the joy at finding the Rodans vanishes from Lucas's face in a heartbeat. "They're gone. Lady Aisling captured them."

Cary leans back against the wall, and for a moment I fear she is about to weep again. But this time, her features harden even as the light in her eyes dims. "Then what are you doing here?"

"We were hoping you and your family could help *us*," I say.

"We need to rescue my parents," Lucas says. "We've been searching for other talented children to convince their families to help."

"And that's not all. The Cerelia Comet returned twelve years too early just the other day. We think it is Lady Aisling's doing. We need to find the sky shaker under her control and get them to set the skies right before other objects are thrown out of alignment."

Cary's expression shifts at the mention of the comet. "Wait a minute. What happened?"

I swallow hard. "Dar tried to warn us. We thought it was just another ploy, but then the Comet appeared, and not long after, Lady Aisling's men came for us."

Cary frowns. "Who is Dar?"

I'd nearly forgotten that the Rodans never did witness the full depth of my betrayal so many months ago, or the real reason why. I quickly explain, and Cary rolls her eyes, reminding me of the girl we met before.

"So far, your family is the only one we've found intact," Lucas says.

The resolve on Cary's face cracks, and as soon as it does,

the truth punches me deep in the gut. But I don't dare say it out loud. I don't want it to be true.

Cary licks her dry lips as her hands squeeze into fists. "I'm afraid you're mistaken. You have not found our family intact. Not even close. Come inside." She gestures for us to enter the dark hall as she closes the door behind us, spinning some kind of lock on a dial.

Lucas stumbles inside, his face pale as moonlight. "Doyle? Is he...?"

"Gone," she whispers. Lucas hangs his head, and I put a hand on his shoulder. Doyle was a good friend of his, a wind whistler. I liked him very much. The thought of him trapped in Lady Aisling's garden is horrible.

A small torch flares on the wall, and Lucas instinctively tugs the light with us as Cary leads us into her home. At first, it is just a long, dark hall, but then it brightens, and we enter a living room with smooth stone walls and chairs carved from the rock. A bookcase is carved into one side too—the middle shelf has sheet music and a few flutes, pipes, and other wind instruments.

Doyle's, no doubt. My heart aches again.

"Where are your parents?" I ask at the same time Lucas says, "What happened to your brother?"

Cary snorts and sinks onto a chair. "Oddly enough, the same story will answer both questions."

Lucas and I exchange a wary look and settle into chairs while Cary fidgets with her sleeves.

"At first the move here was great. We had a new home that was secure. We thought we were safe." She huffs. "We should've known better. A few weeks ago, someone knocked on our door just like you did. My parents assumed it had to be someone from the network. How else would anyone know our house was here?"

"It's cleverly hidden," I say.

"Not cleverly enough," Cary says. "My parents found a woman on our doorstep with a serving boy in tow. I was a few feet behind my parents, so she didn't notice me. She claimed to be a traveler thrown off her path by a storm who was now seeking shelter, but I could sense something was strange right away. I thought my parents could too, but when she reached through the doorway and touched each of their arms, something changed."

"How so?" Lucas says, frowning.

"Their minds. They agreed to let her in. She barely gave me a second glance, but the moment she saw Doyle, she fawned over him. And Doyle loved the attention. There were no guards, no hint anyone would take him by force like we'd heard the Lady's hunters were doing." Cary violently wipes a stray tear off her cheek. "It's…it's my fault Doyle is gone. But I trusted my parents knew what they were doing. And the woman seemed so innocent and young, not at all what I'd expected."

I place a comforting hand on her arm. "I'm sure it's not your fault, Cary."

She shakes her head vehemently. "Oh, no, it is. I'd been quarreling with Doyle all day. I don't even remember what it was about. But I got annoyed when he began showing off his talent and at how much praise he was getting from our visitor, and I went to bed early. The next morning, he, the woman, and her servant were gone."

Cary takes a deep breath and rubs her arms. "If I had stayed up, if I'd been paying more attention, I could've done something. I could've seen the woman for who she really was."

Horror seeps into my skin, as unshakable as a shadow. "Lady Aisling," I whisper.

Cary's face darkens. "She clouded their minds somehow, and it hasn't faded. They've been acting oddly ever since. Their memories of Doyle fade with every day. All I know is if I'd been awake, I'd never have let her take him."

"Cary!" calls a voice I recognize as Mrs. Rodan's. "Dinner's ready!" She sounds completely normal, like nothing strange has happened recently. Like her son did not just up and disappear.

"Just a minute!" Cary calls back.

I shudder. "What did they say about where Doyle went?"

Cary shrugs. "Not much. I don't even know if he went willingly or was forced. The guards may have descended right after I went to bed and dragged him off." She curls her knees up to her chest.

I remember when I first met Cary, she always seemed a little annoyed by her brother and bored with his talent. I almost thought she might have been a little jealous, especially when the three of us were working on our talents together and all she could do was watch.

But now all trace of resentment is gone, leaving only regret and guilt in its wake. The urge to put a comforting arm around her shoulders is strong, but I doubt she'd appreciate it from me.

Lucas is lost in his own world too. I'm not sure what to do with the pair of them. He's been moved around so often by his parents that he doesn't have many friends, and Doyle was one of the few.

But before the heavy silence stretches too long, Mrs. Rodan appears in the room. A smile breaks over her face when she sees me and Lucas. "Lucas! Emmeline. How nice of you to stop by. You must stay for dinner." She glances around with a confused expression on her face. "Are your parents here too?"

Lucas and I shift uneasily in our seats. We don't want to lie, but I'm wary, knowing that Lady Aisling did something to their minds. Only Cary seems safe to confide in.

"They're staying over in the nearby village. We heard you were close and wanted to say hello."

This answer seems to satisfy Mrs. Rodan. "Of course. Well, how nice. You'll stay for dinner, won't you?"

Lucas answers immediately. "Yes, thank you."

Part of me wants to say no, that it would be best to move on to the next house. Staying is too depressing. But then my stomach growls. It's been hours since our last meal.

I suppose having a bite to eat wouldn't hurt. And perhaps

we can dig a little deeper into the mystery of what happened to Doyle while we're at it.

"Thank you," I say. "That would be lovely."

Cary gives us a half smile as her mother retreats down the hall.

"Come on," Cary says. "I'll show you what I mean about them being different now."

CHAPTER FOURTEEN

ary leads us down a dark tunnel that branches off the living room, brightened by the light Lucas brings with him. She leads us into a kitchen and an adjoining room with a table and several chairs.

Mr. Rodan is already at the table, having just set down a plate of vegetables and rolls. He nods at us in greeting. All trace of the disdain they felt for me the last time I saw them is gone. I wonder if they even remember how much danger I accidentally put them in.

I'm beginning to see what Cary means about them being different. All the suspicion, the weight of it, that they carried before, has vanished. They seem free and light—and in some ways, empty.

That slip of paper with the warning *Beware the hollow dolls* springs to mind.

Lucas takes a chair, and I sit next to him, rubbing my arms. I want to pull close a shadow or two, but I don't feel comfortable using my craft around them. It's already too late to tell Lucas not to show off his light singing.

We'll stay here for dinner, but I'm not convinced it's wise to spend the night.

Mrs. Rodan and Cary take their seats too, and we begin to eat. The food smells wonderful—roast potatoes, chicken, and steamed carrots and green beans like the ones Lucas and his mother grew in their garden. The taste sours in my mouth at the thought. If Miranda and Alfred were here, they would know what to do. They'd know what was wrong. They might even know how to get the Rodans to snap out of whatever Lady Aisling has done to them.

Instead, it is only me and Lucas hoping to stumble upon the right answer.

The Rodans are oddly quiet while we eat, nothing like the happy banter I recall from their visit to Lucas's cottage in

Parilla. Instead they smile absently, seemingly oblivious to the disappearance of their son.

I can stand the silence no longer. It feels too grim here without Doyle to break it.

"So, where is Doyle?" It's probably the worst question I could ask, but I'm too tired to be anything other than straightforward. Cary's mouth drops, but the edges curl up in a smile.

Her parents frown, almost like they're puzzled. Like it's a struggle to remember who Doyle is. Then Mrs. Rodan brightens. "Oh, Doyle, yes of course. He is in Zinnia. He was recruited ages ago for a special institute for particularly bright children. He's doing wonderfully there. They keep him busy!" She laughs, no sign whatsoever that this institute is the same ruse that terrified her only a few months ago.

"Yes, we're proud of Doyle," Mr. Rodan says. "I'm surprised you remember him, Emmeline. He's been away for so long I didn't realize you two had met."

Now my mouth drops open. Cary raises an eyebrow. This is exactly what she was talking about. Their memories have been altered.

"But he hasn't been gone long at all," Lucas objects.

"He was with you when you visited us in Parilla not three months ago!"

The Rodans' puzzled expressions reappear, but only fleetingly. Mrs. Rodan pats Lucas on the arm. "That was much longer than three months ago, dear. Had to be a year or two at least."

"Yes, this has been our home for quite some time now. We hardly ever leave. Though Doyle will visit again when he is done with his schooling. We wouldn't want him to take a break just to come home. It is too important."

"Yes," Mrs. Rodan says. "He is very special. And he writes us all the time how happy he is there."

"He writes to you?" I remember the tree house and the letters we saw there. "I'm surprised he has time, if he is so busy."

"Oh yes," Mrs. Rodan's face lights up. "He is a good, thoughtful boy. Let me show you." She leaves the room, and returns a few moments later carrying several papers in her hands. "I'm sure he'd be happy to write to Lucas too, if he had your new address. I know he is fond of you, dear." She hands us the letters. Lucas looks like he is about to be ill.

Together, we read the first letter:

Dear Mum and Dad,

Zinnia is the most beautiful place. The
Lady was right; the school is perfect
for me, and I am making many friends.
Thank you for sending me. I am so
happy here! I cannot wait to show you
all I have learned when I come home.

Love,
Doyle

My skin goes cold. This letter is identical to the one we read before, word for word. Lucas lets out a small gasp when he shuffles the letters and pulls out another.

It is exactly the same.

Every single letter in the bunch is the same. The Rodans haven't even noticed.

Cary is right. Something is terribly wrong with her parents. Something Lady Aisling did. And it is something Lucas and I shall have to find a way to undo on our own.

CHAPTER FIFTEEN

After dinner, Lucas and I are ushered into a long hallway with another set of rooms. Cary's parents show Lucas the spare room and set up a cot for me in Cary's. It's the same as how we slept when they visited us in Parilla, leaving me with a strange sense of déjà vu. I just hope we don't leave this place the way we did the last time—ablaze and on the run from Lady Aisling's guards. I shiver as I settle on the edge of the cot, watching the Rodans smile and bid us all good night.

As soon as the door closes, Cary drags my cot closer to her bed, making me yelp.

"You need to leave. I don't think it's safe here," she hisses in a low voice.

I'm surprised by how closely her thoughts echo my own. "I agree. We'd hoped your parents could assist us, but it seems they need help too. Help we don't know how to give."

"Now that isn't true."

I frown. "We've barely been able to help ourselves."

Cary smiles, the shadows gathering around her face prettily in the faint light. "Saving Lucas's parents and mine is really the same task."

"What do you mean?" My chest feels tight and itchy, almost like my body has figured out what she plans to say before my mind does.

"We're going to defeat Lady Aisling once and for all."

I suck my breath in sharply, the truth of it cutting into me like a knife.

Cary continues. "If what you say is true about the Cerelia Comet, that she risked chaos just to have more power, we have to stop her before those new talented children fall into her hands."

"And before the skies fall apart from what she made the sky shaker do." I smooth my hands over my skirts. "We need to talk to Lucas. I don't know if we can do this on our own, that's why we've been seeking other talented folks and the people who protect them."

Cary grins wider. "Oh, I have a few ideas." Energized, she bounds off her bed and peeks out the door to ensure her parents are nowhere in sight. The hall is empty, and, moments later, she drags a curious Lucas into her room.

He glances between the two of us as he perches on the other end of my cot. "What's going on?"

I shiver again, this time pulling the shadow from the cot around me like a blanket, making it tangible so it has some warmth.

"We're leaving here tonight," Cary says.

Lucas shoots me a confused look. "What do you mean *we*? Your parents are behaving very oddly right now. I don't think it's safe to bring them with us…"

Cary shakes her head. "No, *we* as in you, Emmeline, and I are escaping here tonight."

"Escaping?"

"I can't trust my own parents right now. The way to save both our families is simple: destroy Lady Aisling. Permanently." Cary's hands ball into fists, her eyes flashing with a hatred I've never seen in them before. Even Lucas seems taken aback.

"Destroy her? How? Do you know what she is capable of?" Lucas says.

"All too well," Cary responds.

"How can we possibly defeat someone with so many talents under her command? Maybe we could stop her from taking more talented people and free some of the ones she's captured. But not destroy."

The light of understanding crosses Cary's face. "The comet. Don't you see what that means? She needs more talents. Her supply, it must be running low."

"Running low?" Lucas frowns. "But she has her garden. If her talents are running low, then that must mean…"

"That her 'flowers' are beginning to die." Cary finishes for him. "Which makes this the perfect time to strike. She still has to wait for the new talents. Right now she is at her weakest."

A heady feeling rushes over me. Cary's theory makes sense.

"But that doesn't change the fact she still has more power than we do," Lucas objects.

"No, she doesn't. She can only use one talent at a time. You two are some of the most talented I've ever encountered, and we've seen a lot from our work with the network."

A few months ago, Lucas and I battled Lady Aisling's hunters and Dar, and we prevailed against them both. But we only stopped them temporarily. We won the battle but not the war.

"We need stronger talents. A fire breather or something like that," I say.

Cary laughed. "No, you don't. Trust me, I've been thinking this over for a while now. Even thought I might run away and see if I could find you, but I didn't want to accidentally bring trouble down on your heads. You have powerful talents, you just haven't weaponized them yet."

I shrink back. Dar used my talent as a cover to behave like a weapon herself, and I took the blame for it. I love my shadows—they are good and sweet and dear. I'd never want to use them as weapons. I do not want to hurt anyone. I don't even want to hurt Lady Aisling. I just want her to stop.

Though perhaps those desires are at odds with each other.

Lucas's face contorts. "I'm not sure how I feel about that," he says. "Besides, the most impressive things I can do are toast bread and work with Emmeline's shadows to make a cage." I put my hand over his and he squeezes reassuringly.

"My point is that you both already know how to make your magic tangible. Most talented people don't," Cary says. "All you'd need to do, Lucas, is take it further."

Lucas's brow furrows. "I don't understand."

I confess, I don't quite understand either. I lean forward, curled in my shadow blanket.

"You can toast bread by focusing the light, right?" There is something darkly pointed in Cary's expression.

"Of course, you've seen me do that a hundred times."

"And what does toasting bread entail?"

Understanding dawns, quickly followed a hint of fear. "Heat…" he says softly.

"Exactly. Focus that light more sharply, and it will get hotter. You've been focusing on making your light tangible already, this is just the next step."

Lucas stares at his hands, and the flicker of light he has been absentmindedly rolling over his knuckles goes out.

"I suppose you think I could use that on people. To hurt them if they threaten us."

Cary leans forward, elbows on her knees and a wild light in her eyes. "To hurt Lady Aisling. She won't be expecting it.

But Emmeline here could bind her with shadow ropes while you make the killing blow."

The blood drains from my face. Cary is deadly serious.

Lucas shakes his head. "But I grow things with my light-craft. And bake. I don't think I can use it that way."

I squeeze his hand again, relieved he feels this way too. "Stopping her is one thing. Killing her is another." Suddenly, my mouth runs dry. Little Rose, my childhood friend who made Dar jealous and paid the price. I've been blamed by my parents and neighbors for her death for most of my life, even though it was Dar who led her to her demise, not me. But I gave Dar free rein to do what she wanted, so much of that blame still falls on my shoulders. All the people we hurt with tricks and games—the girl who broke her arm, Kendra's ankle—I don't relish adding more names to that list. "I'm sorry, I can't do it either."

Cary sighs and sits back on her bed. "You're wrong. Stopping her and killing her aren't different things at all. They're one and the same." She hops down from her bed and begins throwing things in a bag she pulls from her bureau. "You'll see that eventually. But for now, we need to leave."

Now that I can agree with. I get to my feet. "Let me see if

your parents are asleep yet." I call the rest of the shadows in the room and swirl them over me, then I swiftly go through the door. The hallway is a well-polished tunnel chiseled from the cliff face, and I make my way back to the kitchen without trouble. There is still a light there. When I peek inside, I find Mr. and Mrs. Rodan awake—at least, I think they are. They sit at the kitchen table, still as statues, staring off into space. Their faces are expressionless. I watch them for several minutes wondering if they will snap out of it.

But there is no change. Not one twitch, nor a single eye blink. I'm not even sure whether they're breathing.

Cold sweat trickles down my spine, and I slink away. When I reach Cary's room, I step inside and release my shadows. My hands quiver no matter how much I try to stop them.

"Are they awake?" she asks.

"Yes, but…there's something strange going on. They're just sitting at the kitchen table, not moving. We can't escape that way. It's too well lit." I reconsider. "Well, maybe they wouldn't notice since they're so still. But I'm not sure we should risk it."

Cary's face has paled, but her jaw is set. "I know another way."

I open the door to Cary's room cautiously, hoping nothing has changed to bring the Rodans down to check on us.

We step into the hall, hearts in our throats, and close the door with a click. The Rodans do not seem to notice the soft noise that sounds like a violent crash to my ears, and we continue on with jagged breaths.

Cary signals which way to go, and I keep to the walls opposite the lights that zigzag down the hall. We pass a couple other rooms and creep by them cautiously, until Cary stops us in front of a dead end. I give her a questioning look, but she raps sharply on the wall without hesitation. The wall creaks far more loudly than I'd like, then sinks outward and opens into the fresh night air.

Cary grins. "Escape hatch. Just in case Lady Aisling ever found us." Her smile falters. "Except I guess it didn't work so well when she did."

"Well, it's useful now," Lucas says.

I balloon the shadows around us as we duck through the exit and steal away into the dark night.

CHAPTER SIXTEEN

With an unusually bright moon to guide us, we spend the rest of the night putting as much distance between the Rodans' cliff home and ourselves as we possibly can. Cary is near frantic to go after her brother. We have to force her to stop when Lucas and I need a rest.

Cary takes the first watch, and Lucas and I fall asleep quickly. A couple hours later, she wakes me with a soft touch on my shoulder. She looks haggard, as though staying in one place allowed her thoughts to catch up with her.

My mind keeps straying back to what Cary said about Lady Aisling's garden wilting. It must be the oldest talents in the garden, the ones she first planted there. After all this time and in spite of all her powers, the flowers can only withstand so much. We must find a way to free them before it's too late. Dar might have been able to help us. At the least, I hope she won't stand in our way.

My thoughts circle and scatter as light begins to inch across the sky. I watch it for a long time, waiting for Lucas and Cary to wake.

←———•———→

Dusk is beginning to shroud the forest when we reach the next home on our list, but the moon above is still as unsettlingly bright as ever. I am not fond of horses—and they're terrified of me—but my feet are sore enough I almost wish we had some right about now. It would make our task much easier and faster.

We approach the house from the west. It's a cottage, settled between tall, close knit trees that remind me of the forest where I first found Lucas. But before we get too close, Cary stops us.

"Hold on," she says. "Listen."

We hover behind a tree, straining to hear. Just when I'm about to give up, I hear it too. Hoofbeats.

Riders, and they're close.

My heart leaps into my throat. "What do we do?" I whisper, glancing toward the house. It must be Lady Aisling's men. I don't want to be caught, but I also don't want to leave the talented person in that cottage to their mercy. Indecision freezes me.

Cary shakes her head. "We'll never get them to safety in time. Quickly, Emmeline, hide us. Then we can follow them and see if there's a way to help them while the guards are sleeping."

I pull the shadow of the great tree we are huddled under around us like a blanket, obscuring us from view. Moments later, the riders with their telltale green cloaks arrive and dismount in front of the cottage. My pulse spikes again as my eyes rove over the group. I'm relieved to see no sign of the cloaked woman or the familiar dirty white dress of Simone among them. If either of them were here, our chances of helping would be severely reduced.

Helpless, we watch the hunters knock on the front door and shove their way inside. The three of us crouch down, listening to the angry shouts of the men and the screams of the parents.

Then silence.

It falls over the forest abruptly, leaving us terrified to move a muscle. We may be hidden, but one snapped twig could give us away if the guards were to hear. My breath aches in my chest as we watch them lead a boy our age with mousy brown hair and wild, terrified eyes out of his home.

"I don't understand! What do you want with me?" He frantically tries to see behind him, but the guard holds him fast. "Why can't my parents come with us?"

The guard hisses something at him and whatever it is, it causes the boy to stop thrashing. My heart sinks. I can't stand watching them take him away from everything he loves, but I can't risk getting caught or putting Lucas and Cary in danger either.

We might be able to delay these men right now if we tried, but I know Lucas and I are both exhausted and not at our strongest. It feels like it's been weeks since we've had a good night's sleep. Plus, there may be more guards ready to swoop in and help if trouble arises.

And the moment we launch an attack, Lady Aisling will know where we are. But if we go with Cary's plan and steal him away under cover of darkness, we can avoid detection. At least, I hope we can.

One of the hunters pulls the boy onto his horse and soon

the platoon is tearing off through the woods. Once they're out of earshot, I can finally breathe again.

"Come on." Cary leaps to her feet. "Let's follow them."

"But what about his parents? Shouldn't we help them?" Lucas says. I feel like I'm being yanked in two directions at once. We need to follow that boy, but if his parents are hurt, how can we abandon them?

Cary huffs. "You can stay if you want, but I'm going after that boy. It sounded like he didn't even know what his talent is." She strides into the woods in the direction of the hunters.

I glance back and forth between the cottage and Cary. Lucas's frown forms a deep *V* on his forehead. "Doyle would never have made a choice like that. He would have stayed and helped the family."

"But what about Cary? We can't leave her either." My head spins as Cary starts to disappear from view.

Lucas grunts. "I guess Cary isn't willing to give us much of a choice." He stomps off after her, and I hurry to catch up with them both.

"Cary!" I hiss. "Wait!" Finally, she spins with her arms folded across her chest.

"Decided to join me? Good. It's the right call."

"It isn't right to leave the parents behind," Lucas says.

She whirls on him. "And it *is* right to leave the boy to Lady Aisling and her hunters? Which do you think will suffer most?" She snorts. "Besides, if they're anything like the other parents you've met, including my own, they've probably already convinced themselves he's happily off to an exclusive school that will do wonderful things for him."

She continues walking at a fast clip. "The parents can fend for themselves. We're not leaving any more kids behind."

CHAPTER SEVENTEEN

e walk in silence for a long time, following the hunters by the wake their horses leave in the dirt. It takes us an hour to catch up to where they've stopped to make camp. Exhaustion seeps through my veins, and I'm sure Lucas feels the same. Cary, however, seems to have an endless supply of nervous energy that keeps her going. We halt at the outskirts of the camp, cloaked in my shadows and looking for sentries. Campfires flicker between the trees, and we edge closer until we reach a spot with a better view of the layout.

We're not far from where their horses are settled down for the night. At least a dozen tents cover this part of the forest, some in the clearing, others spread between trees. A handful of men sit around the main campfire drinking, but aside from their occasional outbursts of laughter, everything is quiet and still.

There is no clear indication of where they are keeping the boy.

"We'll have to check each tent," Cary says, and my heart sinks.

"That's too dangerous," I say.

"What if we get caught?" Lucas says.

"We won't," Cary says. "Emmeline will keep us safe in her shadows."

I hesitate. I do not at all like the idea of peeking into every tent. Sneaking between them to rescue someone tied to a tree like I've done before is one thing—and tricky enough at that—but this is much riskier. What if someone sees a tent flap opening? What if I missed Simone before and she's here, ready to call me out with a single glance?

I clutch my shaking hands together. But if we don't do it, how else will we rescue that boy?

"All right," I say. "But I'll need to go alone. The three of us together is too much potential for noise. And that way if I get caught, you will still have a chance for escape."

"I don't like this," Lucas says, frowning.

"It's for the best," Cary says. "You go on and check the tents while we stay here."

I command the shadows surrounding us to keep Cary and Lucas safely concealed, then take more of the darkness to cover myself as I step away. With a glance back at Lucas, who gives me a small, sad wave, I set out into the camp.

Nerves tingle up and down my spine, and even though I'm safe in my shadows I can't shake the feeling I might get caught at any moment. Simone's ability has shaken my confidence in a way I never thought could happen. But I continue putting one foot in front of the other until I reach the first tent, and then kneel down to peek under the flap. Inside, I spy a few sleeping bodies, but no one who looks like a prisoner. I let the flap drop and move on to the next tent.

I creep around the edges of the camp, checking each tent as I pass, slowly making my way toward the center. At the third, a guard rolls over in his blanket just as I lift the flap to peek inside. I freeze, but he settles down and falls back to sleep. With my heart in my throat, I proceed even more cautiously than before.

As I near the middle of the camp, the feeling of being exposed worsens, crawling over my skin like an army of ants. I stop and hide behind a tree for a few moments to calm myself and keep my breathing even. While the guards cannot see me, they certainly could hear me if I'm not careful. When my pulse returns to normal, I tiptoe toward the next tent. This one is larger than the others, which makes me both hopeful and fearful.

Keeping my shadows close, I crouch low as I creep toward the back of the tent. I kneel and lift the flap. There in the center, tied to the tentpole, is the boy. A guard is also in the tent, and he yawns. If he nods off, that will be my opportunity. Or I could create a distraction. But I fear bringing attention to myself will put Cary and Lucas at risk. I don't want to do that if I can avoid it.

I decide to wait. If morning approaches too swiftly without an opportunity, then I may chance it, but I can't bring myself to do that yet. I peek back into the tent, preparing to hunker down in the shadows for as long as necessary. The boy dozes, but dirt is smudged over his nose and chin, and tears streak his cheeks. I wonder what his life was like before Lady Aisling's men rudely interrupted it. And I wonder if his life, unlike mine, will ever go back to the way it was before.

What could his talent be? Is he truly unaware of it or was that just a ruse?

Though my legs begin to fall asleep, my patience is rewarded after an hour: a shift change.

I hear the second guard before I see him, his steps stirring up dirt and rocks as he stumbles by.

"Hallo!" he says rather loudly into the main tent flap, and I'm glad I chose to use the back flap instead. He would have been right on top of me otherwise. His fellow guard laughs and steps outside.

"Rufus, you've come to take my place? The kid is nothing to worry about."

Rufus laughs. "Have a drink with me first, then. It's going to be a long night."

The first guard snorts his agreement, and they begin to chat about the last time they were home in Zinnia. This is my chance. Every muscle is taut, and anxiety skitters over my shoulders as I creep into the tent. The boy is stirring from the men's voices, and when I'm right next to him, I risk letting my shadows down. I put a finger to my lips as his eyes widen.

"I'm here to help," I whisper. Quickly, I undo his bonds,

and then help him to his feet. I cloak us both in shadows and lead him from the tent. We pause outside just to be sure the guards are still talking.

"Stay close and quiet, and they won't see us," I whisper in the boy's ear. He seems skeptical but doesn't object. Adrenaline throbs through my veins as we tiptoe through the camp, spiking when a cry goes up from the drunken guard once he realizes his charge is missing. The boy frantically glances behind, his breath sharp and heavy.

"It's all right," I whisper, placing a reassuring hand on his arm. "They can't—"

Guards begin to pour from their tents, and something in the air around me changes.

My shadows vanish.

Shocked, I stand there for a moment, staring dumbly around us.

"There he is!"

Panic spurs my feet to move, and I try to gather more shadows as we run from the camp. They slip through my hands like water. I don't understand what is happening. Never before have shadows disobeyed my call.

But I can't worry about that now. We just have to *run*.

We duck and weave, losing the guards momentarily as we enter the woods. I try not to lead them to where Lucas and Cary hide, but they must be close by and watching. As we pass by not far from where I left them, a brilliant flash of light goes up. The guards chasing us cry out and reel back from the blinding light.

Thank the comet for Lucas. At least his magic is still working.

More guards leave their tents every second, and I double back for Lucas and Cary, dragging the boy with me. Now that they've exposed their location, I can't leave them behind. Before we reach them, the light transforms into something extraordinary. Lucas's light singing takes the moon and starlight, twisting it into a high wall that flares out and encircles the camp. I'm willing to bet he has gone and made it tangible too, tacky and thick and not easy to pass through.

When I see Lucas, I can't help grinning. "That was brilliant," I say, and he grins back.

"We need to leave before they get through that," Cary says.

Without bothering with introductions, we flee, the trees flying past as we run. But that feeling of eyes crawls over my skin just like it did in the camp. A branch snaps nearby, and I whirl, bumping into Lucas in the process. No one stands behind us, and I start to breathe again.

"Emmeline!" Cary hisses. My breath stutters in my chest. A boy our age stands in our path. He is taller than Lucas and looks like he hasn't eaten for days. His clothes are ragged and his dark, curly hair a mess. Something about the way he moves reminds me of Simone. There is a hollowness to his sunken cheeks, but his eyes are aflame with a strange light.

One I recognize—Simone had the same light when Lady Aisling took over her body.

I back away. "Run," I whisper. "In any direction. He must be one of Lady Aisling's shells."

But before we can scatter, a cry pierces the night and a burst of white slices through the air, descending on the boy. He doesn't even cry out when talons drag across his face, leaving marks deep enough to make me wince. It's an owl, and it's decided to release its fury.

We don't stick around to ask questions. While the boy—and Lady Aisling—are distracted, we head out into the night careful to cover our tracks as best we can.

CHAPTER EIGHTEEN

Once we are a good distance away, we stop to catch our breath. No sounds of pursuit reach us, and for the moment, I relax. Though I still keep an ear trained for anything out of the ordinary.

I can't say for certain, but I suspect that well-timed owl might have been Dar. It's the only explanation that makes sense. Though what she's doing here I can't hazard to guess. Hopefully it doesn't mean Lady Aisling herself is close by.

The rescued boy wearily sinks onto a nearby log. His eyes water with what I suspect are unshed tears. There is a rip in the knee of his trousers, though I don't recall him falling on our way here. Perhaps that occurred during his capture by the guards. I've been going over our flight in my head ever since we escaped, and I have a suspicion I know what this boy's talent is. My shadows faded when the guards scared him—I'm willing to bet he's the talent taker Lady Aisling has been hunting. But before I say anything, I want to be sure he's not enchanted like so many of the people we've encountered.

"Thank you," the boy says. "But who are you? How did you know I'd been taken?"

I sit next to him. "I'm Emmeline. And this is Lucas and Cary," I say, gesturing to each of my friends.

"I'm Noah."

"We've been trying to avoid those hunters ourselves," I say.

"And we were looking for you and your parents," Lucas adds. "We got to your house just as Lady Aisling's men arrived."

Noah frowns, genuinely confused and without a trace of the far-off look the bespelled people have had in their eyes. "But what do you want with us? And who is Lady Aisling?"

My heart sinks. Could we be mistaken, or has his memory been altered too? Could this boy not be talented after all and just happens to have reclusive parents who moved in after the previous occupants left? Since he's the first we've reached in time, that would be heartily disappointing.

"You really don't know?" Cary says. Exasperation creeps into her voice. She was hoping this might be the lead we needed too.

Noah shakes his head, eyes wide.

"Lady Aisling is a noblewoman from Zinnia. She…" I pause, uncertain how to phrase this without scaring him. But really, he should be scared. "She collects talented children and steals their magic."

Noah's frown deepens. "Then what does she want with me?"

"Don't you have a talent?" Lucas says.

The boy shakes his head. "Nah, I'm pretty boring." His eyes light up. "Why? Do you guys have talents?"

If the Lady made Noah forget about his powers, it may not be safe to share ours, but Lucas responds before I can warn him.

"We do," Lucas says. "I'm a light singer and Emmeline is a shadow weaver."

"Amazing! So that's how you blinded those guards and cloaked us for a bit." He laughs nervously, then looks at Cary. "What about you? What's your talent?"

Cary scowls and folds her arms over her chest. "I don't

have one. I wasn't born in the right year for the comet." Her expression softens with a hint of sadness. "But my brother has a talent. He's a wind whistler."

"Where's he?"

My stomach flips, but Cary responds with a set jaw. "Lady Aisling took him. We're going to save him."

Noah doesn't say anything to that, he just nods.

What are we going to do with this boy? Either I'm wrong and he's talentless, or he's dangerous. I'm glad we rescued him, but I fear he will become a liability. And one more person to look out for. Cary can take care of herself, but we don't know anything about Noah.

"So, if you're not talented," Lucas says, still puzzled, "why were you and your parents hiding out in the middle of the woods?"

Noah shrugs. "My parents have always been weird. And overprotective. I don't think they trust anyone."

"Have you ever heard of something called the network?" Lucas presses.

Noah tilts his head. "No. Why?"

"Just curious." Lucas pauses. "How are your parents weird?"

Noah laughs. "They don't let me go anywhere. Do you know this is the farthest I've ever been from home? If I weren't worried about my parents, I'd almost be enjoying this." He casts his eyes down and picks at a stray leaf. "But mostly I just want to go home. I hope they're all right." He glances hopefully up. "Did you see what happened to them?"

A knot tightens in the pit of my stomach. I wish we had helped them right away like Lucas and I wanted to. Because now, we have no answer for Noah.

"No, we took off after you right away," I say.

"Oh." Noah goes back to picking at the leaf.

"But we can bring you back home if you want—" I begin to say.

"We most certainly cannot," Cary interrupts. "It's too dangerous. That's the first place they'll hunt for you. You're better off with us for the time being."

"I don't understand. Why do they believe I'm special like you? It doesn't make any sense."

"Your parents. How were they weird and overprotective? Exactly what did they do?" I ask. I'm beginning to think Noah's parents knew and never told him he's talented. It would explain a lot.

"Well, they never let me leave the house alone. I could

never go into town, never really saw many people my age. We had a visitor or two once or twice over the years, but they always ushered them out of the house as soon as possible." Noah shrugs. "I always assumed they didn't really like people much."

"Did they ever make you hide if strangers came to the door?" I ask, and Lucas gives me a sharp glance.

"Yeah," Noah says, eyes lighting up. "They did once. Maybe a year ago? It was real strange. Someone knocked on our door, and my mother dragged me into the kitchen and made me hide behind this trapdoor inside the cupboard. They made me stay in there for at least a half an hour after the stranger left too."

My pulse begins to rush. I'm right. I know I am. I smile. "Noah, you *are* talented."

"But that's impossible. I've never used magic."

I grin more broadly. "Actually, you have." I turn to Lucas and Cary. "When I was leading Noah out of the camp something bizarre happened. All of my shadows disappeared. That's how the guards saw us." I gesture to Noah. "But they only disappeared when I was holding on to you."

Lucas's eyes go wide. He regards Noah with awe and a hint of fear. "You're the talent taker they've been hunting."

"The what?" both Cary and Noah say at the same time.

"A talent taker," Lucas explains. "Someone who can cancel magic. That's your talent."

"We overheard some of Lady Aisling's guards talking about how desperately she wants to find one. Somehow she found out about you, and I'm willing to bet your parents knew about it too."

"That would explain why they kept you hidden," Cary says.

"How could I go so long without knowing? And, if I did stop your shadows, I haven't the slightest idea how." Noah shrugs helplessly. "It wasn't on purpose."

"Well, you haven't been around talented people much, have you?" Lucas says.

"I guess not," Noah agrees. "How do I control it? I didn't mean to ruin your magic, Emmeline, and I definitely don't want to do it again." He shudders. "If I can really do this at all."

I glance around. We've been in the same place for too long. The sun has not yet come up, but it will soon, and I'm sure those guards have found a way through Lucas's light wall by now.

"We should keep moving," I say, getting to my feet. "But

we can test out your talent while we walk. I have a feeling we can help you figure out how to use it. And, more importantly, how *not* to use it."

Once we've explained our mission to Noah, we decide to give one more house in the stack of deeds a try. We check our orientation on the map to ensure we're on course. Then we put as much distance between ourselves and our pursuers as possible, while Lucas and I help Noah learn about his magic. At first, he's still doubtful he has any talent at all.

"You did it by accident before. Let's see if you can do it on purpose. This time without touching me. Try thinking really hard about removing my shadows," I say, pulling some of them around me. Noah gasps as my legs disappear in smoke as the shadows curl around them.

Lucas laughs. "Don't worry, I'm still not used to that yet either," he says. "And I've known Emmeline for months."

Noah grins back. "All right," he says. "I'll try." He squints at me, his brow furrowing in concentration. But I keep weaving my shadows, slowly winding them around me. Nothing forces them away or interrupts my magic even for a moment. Finally, he sighs in frustration.

"Maybe you're wrong," he says. "I don't seem to be able to do much of anything."

I put a hand on his shoulder. "We'll figure it out. I'm sure you have magic. There's no other reasonable explanation."

Lucas and Cary gape at us. I frown, but before I can ask them what's wrong, I understand.

My shadows have vanished. Again.

"Looks like touch is definitely the key to making your magic work," Lucas says. "When you touch someone or something with magic, it breaks the spell."

Noah's eyes widen. "How am I supposed to keep *that* under control?" He puts his head in his hands. "What if we run into the guards again, and I bump into one of you while we flee? I'll put you all in danger."

"He's not wrong," Cary says. I shoot daggers at her.

"It isn't your fault, Noah," I say. "There must be a way to control your power. And the effects seem to be temporary, so no harm done."

"We'll help you figure it out," Lucas says.

"And in the meantime, don't touch either of them if we run into those guards again, all right?" Cary says.

Noah sniffles. We keep moving, hoping no one dangerous is on our trail. First Dar's escape, now a boy who can render us powerless without a second thought? The world is quickly becoming a far more dangerous place than I ever imagined.

CHAPTER NINETEEN

It's discouraging that we've arrived at nearly every house too late, though our successful rescue of Noah is a bright spot. Both Lucas and Cary are ready to storm Zinnia without more help, but I can't help feeling uneasy.

It's too much like walking into a lion's den.

Especially with Dar out there doing who knows what. For all I know, she's already been to Zinnia, and my face may be marked as wanted. Though if she was the owl who distracted that boy for us, perhaps not. I don't know what to make of that yet.

As we walk through the woods the next day, I work with Noah on his talent. He was still up practicing when I took over the watch from Lucas last night. I remember seeing something about talent takers in the history book Alsa gave us, and I look it up. Talent takers are dangerous. They can reverse spells, and with practice and concentration they can remove a talent entirely. While this came in handy in the past for obnoxious talents, like bug bringers or stench summoners, the prospect is terrifying for others.

"I'll never figure this out," he says, kicking a stray branch. "Maybe my talent just can't be controlled."

"Of course it can. Any talent can be controlled. But it will take more than a couple hours of practice to do it. Just keep trying." I sigh. "This time why don't you try visualizing pulling your magic inward, toward your body? That might help."

"Is that what you do?" he asks.

"Well, no. I do the opposite when I use my magic. I think of my talent as a force that can reach out and pull the shadows toward me. So, if you do the opposite to keep your talent from working when you don't want it to, that might help."

Noah gives me a thoughtful, though exasperated look. "All right. I'll try anything at this point."

He closes his eyes to concentrate, but quickly opens them again as he stubs his toe. "Ow!"

"Well, maybe don't close your eyes," I say.

Noah cracks a smile. "I guess that would be a little safer. Should I test on you?"

"Not yet. Practice pulling it in for a while, then when we stop for lunch, we can test it out."

While Noah may be frustrated by his lack of progress, he gives it a good try and takes it seriously. All the while, shadows cast by the trees dance over his furrowed brow.

Lucas, though willing to make small talk, has been keeping his distance from Noah. The light is too tempting for him. Even now, Lucas hums and bits of light spark behind his ears and crown his head. When we meet other talented folks, like Doyle, Lucas loves to show off and see how we can use our talents together. But he's different with Noah.

When we stop to rest, Noah sits next to me, rubbing his arms. "Have you noticed the moon is still out?"

"What?" Cary frowns and peers between the foliage.

The moon, which was unusually bright last night, still hangs over our heads. It's markedly bigger than before, as though it draws closer in order to rival the sun for control of the sky. The damage Lady Aisling did to the skies is spreading. We're running out of time.

"The sky shaker," Lucas whispers.

"It's part of the fallout of the Cerelia Comet being moved into a new path, and one of the many reasons we need to stop Lady Aisling," I say. "And soon, before anything gets worse."

Noah shivers. "It's creepy. I mean, it's only the moon, but it just seems wrong for it to be competing with the sun."

I sneak a glance at Lucas to gauge his reaction. Is he stronger because of this new source of light during the day? Or is it a distraction, the wrongness of it changing his usual lovely daylight? His expression does not betray his thoughts.

"Anyway," Noah says, "I've been trying to hold back my talent, but I don't know if it's working."

I swallow my bite of sandwich given to us by Cheyenne's parents, then get to my feet. "Let's find out."

"Good luck," Cary says as she and Lucas watch.

I craft a shadow butterfly that wings through the air toward Noah. It's tangible enough that he should be able to touch it if he wants to. He takes a deep breath, then holds out his hand. The butterfly alights on his thumb. It remains there for a few seconds before disappearing into smoke. The smile that had just been forming on Noah's lips vanishes.

"I'm sorry, Emmeline, I don't know if I can do this."

"Noah, that's wonderful progress! Don't be so hard on yourself. One step at a time."

"Yeah," Cary says. "Until yesterday, you didn't even know that you had a talent."

"It took me years to master my light singing," Lucas adds, then frowns. "Though I suppose that's not helpful, is it?"

"You didn't have other talented people to help you. But Noah does. You've managed to hold back your talent for a few seconds. That's a step in the right direction. Keep practicing. Maybe this time, try to focus on using your talent instead of not using it."

Noah's eyes widen. "You want me to try to remove your talent?"

Nerves tie my stomach up in knots, but he needs someone to help him practice. "Yes, but just for a little while. Don't concentrate too hard, but be intentional with your talent this time."

Noah nods as I gather the nearest shadows into a cloak. He puts a hand on my shoulder and closes his eyes. At first, I don't feel anything much as my shadows dissipate, but after a moment, a tingling sensation begins to burn through my shoulder. Panic rises up my throat, and I shrug him off a bit harder than I mean to.

"All right, that's enough," I say.

"Did it work?" he asks.

I call my shadows to me—and they don't respond. Dizziness overtakes me, and I can't seem to get enough air into my lungs. I sit on a nearby rock, trying desperately not to show the fear roiling inside my chest.

"Yes. Yes, I believe it did," I manage to choke out. I try to call my shadows a second time—still nothing. My skin turns cold. I remind myself that the effects are temporary. They *have* to be temporary.

After one excruciating minute, I call my shadows a third time, and to my relief, they respond.

"Oh thank goodness," Noah says, visibly relieved. "I was afraid I might have done some permanent damage."

I let out a nervous laugh. "Did you feel anything when you were focused on using your talent?"

"I think so. It was almost like I could feel the heat of your magic. And I took away some of that warmth."

"Just be sure you never take away all that warmth," Lucas says. "Unless there's a really good reason."

"And maybe keep practicing on your own with that for now," I say, and they laugh.

We spend a little while longer working on his talent before we decide we need to keep moving again. By the end of it, Noah managed to hold his talent back for a full thirty seconds. And we've discovered when he touches something made from magic—like my shadow butterfly or a spell—it does away with them completely. But talents themselves are harder to remove. It will take much greater control for him to remove a talent entirely as Alsa's history book claims talent takers can do. Noah is still discouraged, but I'm hopeful. We've made progress. I need to think of a way to help him understand that it's all right.

But for now, we pack up the remains of our lunch and hurry on our way. The last house on our list is not hard to find, though we soon discover the reason why. Our knock on the cottage in the midst of a large village on the outskirts of Parilla is greeted by a man and a woman. When asked about a child who lives with them, they become puzzled.

"Child?" the woman says, frowning at her husband. "No, we do not have any children. I'm afraid you must have the wrong house."

I peek into my bag to check the deed again. There is no mistake; this is the right house.

"Are you certain?" Lucas says. "We had heard that a talented girl or boy lived here."

The man laughs. "Talented? Certainly not. That would be something though, wouldn't it?" he says to his wife.

She laughs too. "I am sorry we can't be of more help, but it's very late. Why don't you come in and share our supper? Do you have a place to stay the night?"

The four of us exchange a look. "Not yet," I admit. Like the other houses, they do not question the fact we're on our own without parents. That alone hints of Lady Aisling's hand here.

"Then you must stay here. We may not have children of our own, but we do like having them around," the woman says. "I'm Martha and this is Michael."

"It is nice to meet you," Lucas says. "Thank you for offering to let us stay."

We follow them inside, but something about them, or maybe the house, troubles me. Martha and Michael lead us into a dining room and offer us seats. There are several chairs at the table, which seems odd if it is usually just the two of them.

"Please sit. We already ate, but we'll bring you some leftovers and you can eat while we finish tidying up."

"Thank you, that's very kind," I say, and Lucas, Noah, and Cary murmur their thanks as well.

"We're happy to do it," Michael says, as he follows his wife from the room.

"We'll have to knock on other doors tomorrow morning, I guess," Lucas whispers once they're out of earshot.

I shake my head. "No, I'm positive this is the right house."

"That doesn't make any sense," Cary says.

"Something is wrong here," I say, twisting my hands in my skirts.

"Should we really stay the night?" Lucas asks.

"Definitely," I say. "We're too exhausted to find another place to stay this late, and leaving now would make them suspicious of us. Besides, I want the chance to look around after they've gone to bed and see if there's any sign of a talented child."

Noah shrugs. "They seem all right to me."

"But why are there so many chairs, if only two people live here?" I ask.

Cary raises an eyebrow, but no one else responds, because Martha returns carrying a plate of roast chicken with vegetables and potatoes. The wonderful smell makes my mouth water.

She leaves the food behind, and we don't wait to tuck in. It tastes as good as it smells, and soon our bellies are full again.

We gather up our dishes and bring them into the kitchen to find Martha and Michael standing there doing...nothing. Not even their shadows twitch. That is until they see us and suddenly brighten up.

"Oh, thank you for helping clean up, dears," Martha says. "Michael, will you show them where they can sleep?"

He leads us down a hallway at the back of the kitchen toward the living room. "I was just remarking to my wife how nice it is to have children here. You are welcome to remain as long as you like." He smiles at us, but it doesn't quite reach his eyes, almost like he's a marionette and someone else is pulling the strings. My heart trips over itself.

When we reach the living room, Michael sets up several cots while Martha brings some blankets for us.

"Make yourselves at home. If you need anything, we'll be just down the hall."

We thank him and regroup on the cots.

"Does it seem odd to you that they set us up here in the living room?" Lucas asks, wrinkling his nose.

"It does," I say. "This house is big enough that they must have at least two bedrooms."

Noah shakes his head. "Maybe this really is the only place they have for guests. They didn't have to invite us to stay, you know."

"Or maybe they did it to keep an eye on us," Cary says. Noah rolls his eyes. He is not yet as suspicious as the rest of us. He will be soon enough.

"There has to be a child's room here. I'm sure of it." I get to my feet, already calling my shadows. They swirl around me until they conceal me from head to toe. I peek out into the hall.

"Emmeline!" Lucas hisses. But it is too late. I'm already sneaking down the hall counting the doors. Martha and Michael are still awake, making it too risky to investigate the rooms, but the existence of a child's bedroom would bolster my theory. Two doors lie at the end of the hall, directly across from one another. I am dying to open them, but Martha or Michael moves around in the one on the left. One creaky hinge would give me away. If something is going on here that has to do with Lady Aisling, revealing my talent is the last thing I should risk in this house.

I sigh, giving the doors a last long look, and creep back to the living room where my friends wait. Cary, Noah, and Lucas are wide-eyed when I return and release my shadows. Lucas breathes an audible sigh of relief.

"Emmeline, we need to be more careful," he says.

"I was careful." I settle on a cot again. "There are two bedrooms. But I couldn't go in. Martha or Michael was moving around in one."

"Why would they put us up in the living room if there's a perfectly good bedroom available?" Noah asks.

"Now that is an excellent question," Cary says.

Puzzled and more discouraged than ever, we each take one of the four cots. Lucas and Noah are snoring within minutes, but Cary and I both lay awake for a while.

"Something doesn't feel right here," Cary says after a few minutes.

"I know. I feel it too."

Martha or Michael bustles around the kitchen for a little while longer, before retiring to their bedroom. Cary eventually falls asleep too, her chest rising and falling in a steady rhythm. But for me, the odd sense of being watched that has followed me since the moment we set foot in this place intensifies, making sleep impossible.

A snapping sound sends me shooting bolt upright. I glance around, but all I see are shadows and the sleeping forms of my friends. Then something materializes in the corner of the room. Something I swear wasn't there before.

It's gone as quickly as it appeared.

I rub my eyes, wondering if perhaps I'm more tired than I realized, and this is all just a strange hallucination, when I hear that *snap* again. This time a figure appears directly beside me.

Before I can yelp, the figure puts its hand over my mouth and whispers in my ear, "Please, don't scream. I didn't mean to scare you. I have to be extra cautious."

Wide-eyed, I examine the speaker as the hand slides from my mouth. It's a girl about my age with long, straight pale hair in a dress that is either a drab gray or dirty white. Freckles splash over the bridge off her nose and onto her cheeks. Her eyes are just as wide and scared as mine.

"Who are you?" I whisper. "Where did you come from?"

She smiles sadly. "My name is Pearl. I live here. I think you might be looking for me, but you need to leave. Right now."

"What do you mean?" I ask, my pulse beginning to race. If this is a dream, I'm starting to think it's a nightmare.

"Sorry, I overheard you talking about that Lady Aisling woman and seeking out talented folks. I have a talent, like you do. I'm a spot hopper. I can move between two points instantly regardless of the distance between them as long as I've seen the destination or I'm with someone who has seen it. This is my home, my parents, but they've turned against me. And now they've turned against you. Guards are on their way here. You must leave. I'll meet you under the willow tree at the edge of the village. Hurry."

Then she disappears with a *snap*.

I waste no time waking the others. We had planned to wait until morning to leave so that Michael and Martha wouldn't suspect anything, but not anymore. I may not know Pearl yet, but she didn't act at all like Lady Aisling's shells, and her words had the ring of truth. We all agree leaving immediately is the safest course.

Under the cover of my shadows we creep to the window and quietly push it open. The house is one level, so the drop to the ground is short. Just as the last of our feet touch the ground a sharp knock raps on the front door, spurring us to flee like the wind. We don't speak again about Pearl or talents until we're outside the town and certain we have not been followed.

CHAPTER TWENTY

We pause for a brief rest under the giant willow tree Pearl mentioned at the far edge of the village. Between my shadows and the tree's long hanging branches, we are well hidden. We have only been there a few minutes when Pearl appears with a *snap*.

The tension releases from her expression when she sees us. "I'm so glad you got out of there in time. But we shouldn't stay here long. The guards have already begun to search the village."

"Thank you for warning us," Lucas says. We fall into step, covered by my shadows as we enter the forest.

"What happened with your parents?" I ask. "This can't be the first time those guards have been here."

Pearl shudders. "No, it isn't. I don't quite understand how it all happened, but it began when we had a visitor. My parents have always been strict that I must hide when someone we're not expecting arrives at our door. We have a designated spot a mile away. Then I can pop back to check that it's safe when I feel like it."

My breath catches in my throat. Spot hopping is another fearsome talent. No wonder Lady Aisling wanted it. She could collect her prey in minutes instead of months if she could cut out the need for travel.

"That is extraordinary," I say. Pearl's grin is fleeting.

"Your shadow weaving is pretty intriguing too," she says. "When these visitors came, I did what I always have—fled to the designated spot. But it wasn't long before I heard people approaching. I popped just outside the area and saw it was the same men who came to the door." She clasps her hands together. "I didn't know how they figured out where I was hiding, at least not until I hopped back home."

"What happened?" I whisper.

"I traveled into a closet, that way I could hear everything and find out if the visitors were still there before showing myself." She wrings her hands. "I overheard a woman talking to my parents. But my parents sounded strange. Nothing like they usually do. They were assuring the woman I could be found at that spot and if not, then I was bound to come back home any minute." She glances behind her warily. "They were going to hand me over to them. Just like that. But I didn't like the look of this woman, or the servant boy she had with her. Something about them made my skin crawl. And I really didn't like the effect she was having on my parents. I've been hiding ever since."

I wonder if the boy is the same one who nearly caught us as we fled with Noah last night. I suspect he is one of Lady Aisling's shells like Simone, though I can't hazard to guess what his talent is. But it must be powerful if the Lady keeps him close.

"That must have been Lady Aisling. She's awful. She collects people like us and steals their talents. It's a smart thing you hid." I frown. "We've seen several sets of parents after their children have been taken and they're different. Like she's done something to their minds. That must be why they told us that they never had a child when we got here, let alone a talented one."

Pearl shivers. "Thank you for taking me with you. I'm afraid to stay here any longer. If my parents see me, they may try to hand me over again." Tears shimmer in her eyes, and I reach out a hand to comfort her.

"That's why we're here. We've been hoping to find other talented people to help us fight back against Lady Aisling. Lucas's parents were stolen, and so was Cary's brother. And Noah's parents are probably like yours now. We're going to get our families back. Will you help us?"

Pearl's eyes sparkle with a new light now. "Do you think defeating Lady Aisling might undo whatever it is she did to my parents?"

"I hope so." I glance over at Noah. "And if not, we may have another means to help. I can't promise we know exactly what to do, but we have some ideas, and that's a start. Besides, there is safety in numbers," I say.

Pearl smiles at me. "Then count me in."

"Why don't we try to help Pearl's parents now?" Lucas says. "Noah could use the practice."

Noah's eyes widen. "But there are so many guards," he says. "And I've never canceled a spell before."

"You can cancel spells?" Pearl says.

"Sort of," Noah says. "I'm a talent taker. But I just found out."

"Oh," Pearl says, her hope deflating. "The current situation is a bit dangerous for practice. My house is still crawling with guards. I don't want anyone to get caught."

I pat Pearl's arm. "Once Lady Aisling is defeated, we'll come back and help your parents, I promise."

We are all tired, but giddy with excitement. We've now found two people with talents, which only a few days ago seemed an utterly hopeless task. I feel emboldened, like we might actually be able to free them all if we keep at it.

But wariness falls over our little group as we near the border to Zinnia. We're encroaching on enemy territory, and while I'm sure not all Zinnians are evil like Lady Aisling, who knows how many might be under her spell? We must be extra careful to remain undetected in her home territory.

We are going to have to save our friends and as many other talented folks as we can on our own.

The sun and moon are both high overhead, and the long trees cast short stumpy shadows when we reach the border. It's marked by an arched wrought-iron fence stretching as far as the eye can see. There must be an entrance somewhere, but it is nowhere in sight.

Cary sighs, then eyes the iron bars. "We're going to have to climb," she says.

Pearl pushes forward and puts a hand on Cary's shoulder. "Oh, I don't think that will be necessary."

One *snap*, and the two of them vanish. Seconds later they reappear on the other side of the fence. My jaw drops.

"You can bring people with you?" Lucas says, equally impressed.

"Of course. Though we all have to be connected through touch if I want to bring more than one at a time."

Lucas and I hold hands and Pearl brings us over, but has difficulty when it's Noah's turn. Try as she might, she just can't seem to use her talent when she's touching Noah. He concentrates, trying to hold his talent back, but he can't do it for long enough for her to make the jump. It's like his very skin exudes his nullification magic. Before we can decide what to do, a loud cry breaks the silence. We all stop and glance around, but see nothing. Prickles run up and down my back.

Then the cry comes again, loud and piercing.

Pearl pops away, and Noah ducks behind the nearest tree. I grab Lucas and Cary and do the same, weaving my shadows around us, and Noah too. Something is coming, and there is nowhere for us to run. Not without abandoning half our group.

My heart pounds in my throat, but at the third cry, I can't help but peer around the trunk of the tree. A giant shadow lumbers through the trees toward us. Then it shrinks as it gets closer. When I finally see the figure weaving through the trees, my breath catches in my throat.

It's me.

Or rather it's Dar, twisting my mouth into a maniacal grin. She bounds toward us, sprouting huge arms with thick giant hands as she goes.

"Dar, what are you doing?" I say. But she just keeps laughing. When she reaches the bars, Noah cowers behind a nearby tree, but she pays him no mind. Instead, she braces her new hands between the iron bars and pushes them apart until there's a space big enough for her to step through. She grins at me as her hands and arms shrink back to normal size and she leaps through the hole.

"I'm helping, Emmeline. Can't you see?" She gestures to the hole. "Now your friend can get through too." She tilts her head and smiles sweetly, but it reminds me of Simone in a chilling way.

Lucas stands beside me with his arms crossed, but his expression softens a little once he realizes Dar did actually help.

"Thank you, Dar. That was nice of you." I gesture to Noah and Pearl, who has just popped back to that side of the fence out of Dar's line of sight. "It's safe to come out and cross now."

Warily, they approach the gate like it might be poisonous. Pearl steps through first, shy to reveal her power in front of Dar, and Noah follows behind her. They both gape at Dar-Emmeline, glancing back and forth between us.

"Do you have a twin, Emmeline?" Pearl asks us both like she's not sure which of us is really me.

"No," I say at the same time Dar says "Yes."

I give Dar a stern glance. "It's a long story. The short version is Dar was once Lady Aisling's sister. She was the Lady's first victim and became a shadow—my shadow, until I helped her become human again. Her talent is shape shifting."

Dar sprouts the oversized arms and hands to demonstrate. Pearl takes a step back, but Noah inches closer and touches Dar's arm curiously.

Dar instantly shifts, her arms shrinking to normal size and my face fading into one I've never seen before: a girl a little taller than me with brown curls framing her startled expression. Freckles dance across the bridge of her nose. She gasps, her now human hands reaching up to touch her face.

"What…what just happened?" She recoils from Noah, who guiltily pulls his hand back. As soon as he does, Dar shifts again, this time into a bird that shoots to the top of the wrought-iron fence.

"We found a talent taker, Dar," I say. "But he can't fully control it yet."

The bird, cloaked in dark blue feathers, gives me an arch look.

I do my best to put on a stern face. "Now, Dar, what are you doing here? Have you been following us?"

The bird chirps her objection then flies down to alight next to me. Soon I'm staring into my own eyes again. Blue wings still flutter on Dar's back.

"I've been helping you," she says. "Didn't you find what I left for you in those houses?"

"That was you? You're the one who left us those warnings?"

Dar's shoulders slump. "Of course. I promised you we'd always take care of each other. I meant it, even if you didn't." She huffs and folds her arms over her chest. "Besides, I've been doing what I told you I would do if you let me go: scouting out Lady Aisling's weaknesses."

"And what did you find?" Lucas asks.

Her face falls, and her hands begin to fidget. "I'm...not sure anymore. I know I had a plan to defeat her, but when I try to remember what it is, it's just...gone."

"Of course it is," Lucas says, shaking his head. "You never had a plan, did you?"

"What do you mean gone?" I ask.

She ignores Lucas and only answers me. "I've felt different ever since I attacked that hollow boy in the woods."

"The one who almost caught us?" I say. "So you were that owl?"

"He felt like Simone, strange and empty. He's one of Lady Aisling's damaged children. He must be a memory stealer. She has no trouble transforming talents that deal in the physical into flowers, but for some reason, it never goes right with those who have mind-based talents. But as you know from Simone, she still found a way to use the shells."

Cary shudders. "A memory stealer under Lady Aisling's control would explain a lot."

Dar nods vigorously. "Yes! Like why I can't remember my plan. It was perfect too! I was so excited to share it, and now…" She throws up her hands. "But I can still help. I remember everything about my sister, and we can form a new plan to defeat her together."

"I don't know. You haven't been honest with me before. How can we be sure what you say is true?"

She pouts. "I wouldn't lie about my plan."

Lucas frowns. "We need to discuss this without you hovering."

Dar clicks her tongue. "Still so untrusting." But she moves off a few yards, and the five of us huddle together.

"We can't let her come with us," Lucas says. "She's up to something, and she's bound to betray us if it suits her purposes. I don't believe for a second that the boy stole just the right memory. Too convenient."

"Plus, we can't control a creature like that," Pearl says, glancing over her shoulder.

I sigh. "I know controlling her is an issue. But Lucas and I can try to trap her in her cage again if she gets too far out of hand. And for what it's worth, I do believe her about the memory stealer, and she has left us warnings and help along the way. The only way she'd know about it is if she was the one who did it."

Cary eyes Dar suspiciously. "Shape shifters always struck me as the most untrustworthy of talented people."

Noah glances back and forth between us all. "But if she's Lady Aisling's sister, she really is in a position to help us, isn't she? I mean, she knows her. And we know only a little."

"That is true," I say. "If there is one thing we can trust about Dar it's that she will do anything to get revenge on her sister."

"I think we should let her come with us," says Noah. Pearl and Cary consider this.

Lucas sighs exasperatedly. "She'll betray us. In Zinnia that could mean getting caught by Lady Aisling and her men. It's too risky."

But Pearl and Cary seem more willing to give her a chance.

"I don't know Dar, though I can say I don't trust her," Cary says. "But Emmeline makes a decent point. We know she wants to take down her sister—we have the same goal. I don't see any harm in letting her come with us, as long we all keep an eye on her."

"That makes sense to me," Pearl agrees.

Lucas frowns. "Fine, but I still think it will be our undoing."

CHAPTER TWENTY-ONE

Despite Lucas's reservations, Dar proves true to her word. She leads us through the woods surrounding Zinnia in a roundabout way that ensures we do not encounter anyone else.

If I ever doubted she grew up in Zinnia before, I certainly don't now.

Sometimes, though, she seems to forget we are following her and stumbles too far ahead. I keep us cloaked in shadows as best I can, but she makes it difficult to keep up.

It is much harder to keep her in line now that she's no longer tethered to my feet.

In Zinnia there are flowers everywhere. It started in the

woods near the wrought-iron fence, but becomes more notice-able the farther we venture into the territory. Delicate wild-flowers like bluebells, queen's lace, and daisies cast their intricate shadows in the woods and fields, then as we get closer to the main town, they bloom brighter and have more variety, many of which I don't know the names for. It's sad that such a lovely place is lorded over by a cruel, dangerous ruler.

When we approach the town, Dar takes a long way around the city wall to avoid the main entrance. From afar we can see the telltale green cloaks of Lady Aisling's hunters lingering by the gates.

My stomach flips. This is where Simone lives when she's not out hunting. And if that creepy boy—the memory stealer—is any indication, there are others like her just as dangerous.

Dar stops at a point by the wall far enough into the woods that no hunters patrol here as far as I can tell. I breathe a little easier. The wall is too high to see over, crafted from red bricks and covered with creeping vines.

"This is how we can get in." Dar makes a few quick movements I don't quite follow, and a hidden door swings open smoothly.

"How did you do that?" I say.

She grins. "It's a mirage of sorts. Carefully crafted to be nearly invisible. All you have to do is press here, here, and here." She points to three spots on the now open door. "And then it unlocks. Just be sure you do it in that order."

"Can I try?" I ask.

Dar shrugs, her smile dimming as if she's losing interest in this game already—that is when she's at her most dangerous. I'd better be quick. She closes the door, and I press the three spots. I don't quite get it right on the first try, but on the second, the door swings open.

Now it's my turn to grin.

We march through in single file and find ourselves in a back alley, cloaked in darkness and with no idea where we're going.

"What now, Dar?"

She giggles. "Just follow the flowers, and you'll be safe."

I frown as she skips ahead to point at something on the wall. Imprinted into the brick is a many-petaled flower, about half the size of my fist.

"So that's the sign to look for?"

"It will keep you on the fastest route through the back

alleys of the town. I used these all the time when I was a child to sneak out and explore the woods."

Lucas casts around nervously. "Why don't you show us somewhere safe to spend the night? It's getting late."

I'm almost startled to realize he's right. We've traveled much farther than I expected today, but the unnervingly bright moon that refuses to wane makes the days seem longer than they really are. It is huge now, seeming to loom close to the ground and rivaling the setting sun.

"But I've only just begun to show you the good stuff." Dar's face falls, and I intercede.

"Lucas is right. Maybe tomorrow we can come back, and you can show us more."

Lucas and Cary both give me a sharp glance, but I ignore it for now. Keeping Dar happy and stable is important—especially within the enemy's home territory.

She sighs dramatically. "One condition: you and Lucas promise not to try to put me back in that awful cage while I'm sleeping."

Lucas chokes behind me, but I have no choice but to agree to her terms. We need a safe space to spend the night. "Yes, we promise."

She gives us a sly look, then marches back out the secret door toward the woods. I have to hurry my shadows to keep up with her.

"Zinnia wasn't the first town to be built around here, though it did become the one the territory was named after," Dar mumbles more to herself than anyone else. I try to engage her in conversation to find out more.

"What was the other town?"

She shrugs. "No one remembers its name anymore. But the ruins are nearby."

I frown. "They didn't build over it or incorporate it into Zinnia?"

She shakes her head. "Why would they? The ruins were already in shambles when Zinnia was founded."

"And how long ago was that?" Now she has piqued my curiosity—a thing almost as dangerous as Dar's boredom.

"Two hundred years? Maybe more? It was a long time ago when I was a child, so even longer now."

I recall what Alsa told us of Lady Aisling. She was an adult nearly one hundred years ago. These ruins must be ancient.

Without warning, Dar sprints ahead of me, sprouting

wings on her back as she goes. "We're almost there!" she cries, making me wince.

"Dar!" I admonish. "Hold on! And don't yell, please. We don't know who else might be out in these woods. They must have patrols."

Dar laughs and keeps running. The others chase after us. Was I wrong to argue for trusting her even a little? She did get us through the gates and into the town, and provided a means for moving around largely unnoticed. It doesn't make sense that she'd suddenly desert us now.

Of course, not much about Dar makes sense on a good day either.

With my heart in my throat, I follow her, running as fast as I can until my legs ache and my chest burns. Up ahead, I can see she has stopped at the top of a hill. When I reach her, I take in the sight before us while the others catch up.

Below, a valley cuts through the landscape, green coating everything that lies there. Patches of stonework, ancient towers, and gaps from where the wood rotted away reveal a village that long, long ago some people called home.

Dar grins. "See? We can stay here. There is shelter in the

larger building in the center. No leaks or anything. Or at least, there wasn't last I was here." With that, she changes the rest of the way into a bird and soars out over the valley. It happens so quickly I don't have time to object.

Lucas and the others finally reach the top of the hill. They pause behind me, all of them breathing hard.

"What is this?" Cary says.

"Our temporary home," I say. "Let's see if we can find our way down into the valley."

Pearl frowns. "I can bring most of you," she says. "But I don't want to leave Noah out here alone."

Noah pipes up. "I've been working on holding my talent back on the way here. I might be able to do it for long enough."

"I don't know," Pearl says. "I don't think I want to risk my power disappearing in the middle of a hop from such a high point. Let's try a shorter distance when we get there."

"I'm sure there's a path somewhere. We'll all go together," I say.

The sun retreats over the tops of the trees as we make our descent through the thick forest. Eventually we do find a path, and we find Dar sleeping in the large building in the center of the village.

Now that we're closer, the immensity of the ruins is more apparent. There must have been hundreds of people who lived here in the village once. I can't help wondering what happened to them. The stonework is beautiful, with intricate carvings and symbols I cannot place. The way the shadow and light falls through them is lovely, casting strange patterns on the ground and walls. Did they have talented folks too? Perhaps they were the sort of people who once revered those with talents instead of feared them. I would have liked to have seen those days.

Dar snores in a corner on a cloak she must have swiped from my pack when I wasn't looking. I decide not to wake her unless absolutely necessary; we need to make plans, and the less she knows about them the better.

We sit in a circle on the raised stone steps leading up to a platform at the far end of the huge room and share our food supplies. With six of us now, we won't have anything left for breakfast.

"We have to go into Zinnia tomorrow morning at first light," I say. "We need to find their market and buy more food. There's too many of us now."

Lucas nods. "And now that we know to follow the flower

symbols, we can also sneak around and find out more about where the Garden of Souls is located. Then we just need to find a way inside and free as many of the talented folks as possible."

"Especially my brother," Cary says.

"Definitely," Lucas agrees. "And my parents."

"And the sky shaker. We must find them as soon as possible," I say.

"How are we going to free them if they've been transformed into flowers?" Pearl asks. We filled her in on the gaps in her knowledge of Lady Aisling on the journey, but haven't revealed our whole plan yet.

"That's where Noah comes in. If we can get him into the garden, all he should have to do is touch the flowers to undo the magic," I say.

Noah smiles uncertainly. "No pressure or anything."

"The real question is what are we going to do if we can't find a way into the garden? Or if we get caught? Shouldn't we do some research first, then figure out a plan?" I say. Usually Lucas and I are of one mind, but on this point we're not. His parents' capture has made him a little more reckless. Like Cary.

"No, we need to act as soon as possible," Lucas says. "If

Lady Aisling gets wind of us poking around the city before we make our move, she'll have time to prepare."

"I agree. If she finds out we're here, it's over," Cary says. Pearl and Noah murmur their agreement too, but the hard knot in my stomach won't leave me alone. "Besides, we have Noah. He's been practicing. According to that history book, if he keeps at it, he could take away her powers, maybe even permanently."

"Then we need to bring Dar. She can help us find the Garden of Souls quickly, and she knows Lady Aisling and her habits. If something goes wrong, she'd be a real asset," I say.

"Absolutely not!" Lucas hisses a little too loudly. I glance over at Dar, but as far as I can tell, she remains asleep.

"Lucas, she could help us," I say.

But Cary doesn't agree either. "It's too dangerous. Who knows what flight of fancy she might run off on while we're depending on her? What was she thinking in the forest on the way here? Yelling and running then shifting into a bird?"

"Not to mention leaving us behind," Pearl says. "That was just rude."

I sigh. "I know... She can take some getting used to. And I know she's erratic and has a tendency to lie too. But she would do anything to get revenge on Lady Aisling. She might risk everything else, but she would never risk that. If we want to humiliate, damage, or defeat the Lady in any way, she'll help us to the best of her ability."

"Let's vote," Lucas suggests. "All in favor of letting Dar come with us, raise your hand."

Only my hand goes up. The knot in my stomach grows tighter.

"All in favor of leaving Dar here, raise your hand," Lucas says. All four raise their hands.

"Fine, we'll leave her here," I say, though it feels wrong. The others prepare for bed while Noah retreats to a corner to practice. I get out my bedroll for the night, and glance over at Dar again; I can't help thinking I see a glimmer from her open eyes. But when I blink, they're closed. I frown, stepping closer to peer at her. She sleeps soundly, chest rising and falling evenly.

I don't have the heart to wake her just to give her disappointing news. We'll have to tell her she'll be left behind in the morning.

CHAPTER TWENTY-TWO

We manage to leave without Dar—though she is none too happy about it. After I broke the news, she stomped away into the streets of the ruins. She didn't return to the main building before we left, but I know she won't be able to resist hearing about our adventure in the city when we return.

It is a beautiful, sunny day, despite the strangeness of the looming moon. It's so inviting, Lucas can't help but reach out and mold the light to his wishes, rolling tiny orbs over his fingers. But for the most part we have been a solemn bunch. Every once in a while though, I catch Noah grinning at nothing at all, which strikes me as odd. Perhaps he's just pleased with himself since he's finally begun to have some success controlling his talent.

We sneak in through the entrance Dar showed us and head for the market square Dar said could be found in the center of town, using the flower trail to guide us. Venturing into the market is the most exposure we've risked, but we need food; our bellies ache for breakfast. Plus, we need to check out Lady Aisling's estate. That will be the most dangerous part. We must get close, but not close enough to be caught.

I don't have my shadows up to conceal us since we'll have to actually talk to the vendors in order to get the food we need. Fortunately, Lucas and I still have coins left from what Miranda and Alfred slid into our bags the night it all began.

The market here is much larger and livelier than the ones in Parilla and Abbacho. There are rows of vendors and smells and sounds we've never encountered before. One thing in particular is everywhere in Zinnia and is being sold in several carts in the market: flowers. And the most popular flower is the town's namesake with its many-petaled blossoms and bright colors. We can barely walk five feet with seeing one. I suspect this is in some way thanks to Lady Aisling and the rumored beauty of her Garden of Souls.

It certainly casts these otherwise lovely flowers in a very different light.

"This place is enormous," Lucas says.

"We'll need to split up to get what we need quickly," I say. Lucas and I decide to tackle one side while Cary, Noah, and Pearl take the other. Gaily colored banners flap in the wind, their shadows fluttering like strange, dark birds.

We hurry between rows searching for the booths that have what we need, and don't stop for anything else, despite the temptation of a particularly delightful smelling pastry cart. Even though no one knows who we are, and we don't see any familiar faces, I can't help feeling like eyes are crawling over my skin.

It's the same feeling I felt in the forest when that memory stealer crossed our path. I know better than to ignore it. I keep my eyes open, but my fears to myself. As we leave the bakery with a few fresh loaves of bread, a crash rings out from the other side of the market, loud enough to make me whirl around.

"Come on." Lucas grabs my hand and tugs me after him. We duck behind an empty stall, weaving our way through the backs of several booths in this row. We come out near where we should meet the others at the entrance to the market. Cary and

Pearl are waiting for us when we arrive breathless, glancing over our shoulders.

Cary frowns. "What's wrong?" she says at the same time Lucas asks, "Where's Noah?"

"Halt!" cries a booming voice that sends shivers shooting through my body. A group of guards with those all-too-familiar green cloaks chases after a familiar form—Noah—as he races toward us, knocking over everything in his path. At the far end of this row stands a girl with dark hair and skin and a vacant look in her eyes. When she sees us, she tilts her head and steps slowly in our direction. I grab Lucas and shove him forward.

"We need to go," I say. But when we turn to run, we find three other children surrounding us. All the same age, all the same vacant look. How many mind-based talents does Lady Aisling have under her control?

Between the guards and the shells, we're boxed in on all sides. The man at the head of the group, I recognize: Lord Tate's nephew, Alden. Only a few months ago, he chased me for days. I'd recognize him anywhere.

"Run!" I cry, and we sprint in every direction. I set the others' shadows upright, then scatter them to delay the guards, but they are already upon us. One of them grabs my cloak by the hood, and I whip around, managing to wrench it out of his grasp. I duck behind the nearest building and throw up my shadows to blend in with my surroundings, but my breath rasps from fear.

And worse, I don't know how the others are. Panic crawls over me. What if they're all captured and I'm the only one left? I'll have to return to the camp with only Dar to help me.

The guard pokes his head in the alley, clearly surprised to find no one there. I breathe a sigh of relief when he returns to the main thoroughfare.

I peek around the corner and gasp. Pearl is nowhere to be seen. Cary is gone too. Good, maybe Pearl hopped to a safe place with her. Lucas struggles with a guard, trying desperately to use his light singing to free himself. But the guard catches on and clamps a hand over Lucas's mouth.

Without his voice to wield it, his magic is useless.

Another one of the guards has a grasp on Noah, but he slips away, laughing, and runs behind a building. Two guards give chase, including the one who tried to capture me. A shout goes up from behind the building, and they return, dragging a struggling body between them. For a moment, the struggle stops, and a surge of shock jolts through me.

The person they hold is me.

That's not Noah at all. It's Dar. Somehow she switched places with him.

And now she's been caught too.

CHAPTER TWENTY-THREE

snap resounds nearby, and I look up. Pearl stands a few feet behind me in the alley, peering into the shadows. "Emmeline?" she hisses.

I loosen my hold on a few of my shadows so she can see me. "Over here," I whisper.

"We need to leave. I've already got Cary safely away," Pearl says.

"But we can't just abandon Lucas." Something hard and heavy presses on my chest, and I have to swallow the sob welling up in my throat. The thought of leaving him behind... I can't do it. I won't.

"What choice do we have?" Pearl says. "I can't whisk him

away alone while someone else has his hands on him, and I don't think they're about to let him go."

"Maybe we can distract them somehow?" Tears burn the backs of my eyes, but I can still see Pearl shake her head sadly.

"If you have an idea that won't get us caught, let's hear it. But I'm stumped," she says. I can't think of anything that wouldn't thoroughly expose us and our talents. We may have taken on some of the guards before, but an entire city of them is more than I can handle.

Pearl takes my elbow. "If we get caught, we can't help Lucas and…" She trails off.

The guards have pulled Lucas up next to Dar, who is oddly still. Far more still than I'd expect. She's up to something, though I'm not sure what.

Pearl gasps. "Where's Noah?" She glances at me and then back out onto the main thoroughfare. "How…how is that possible?"

"It's Dar. She must have tricked Noah and taken his place with us. She shifted into me when the guards got here."

"Why would she do that?"

I wring my hands, and the shadows in the alley shiver

in response. "I don't know. It's almost like she knew we'd be found out today." My breath sticks in my throat. *Did* she know? Or worse, did she do something so that we'd—*she'd*— get caught? That would explain why the guards were chasing her through the market. Was that her plan all along? If so, why did she need us?

The guards appear to be waiting for something...or someone. Pearl moves to take us back to our hideout, but I hold up a hand.

"Wait a minute."

"We really need to go, Emmeline."

"Just one more minute. Please," I say.

She sighs, the crease on her forehead deepening. "All right, but just one. Then I'm taking you back whether you like it or not."

We don't wait for long. Moments later, more guards arrive. In the midst of them walks a tall woman with a dark green cloak. My insides freeze, and my palms turn slick at her appearance.

I have no doubt that woman is Lady Aisling.

She carries herself as if she owns the city, which of course, she does. Even the guards themselves might be bewitched to carry out her demands of stealing children from their homes. She lets her hood down when she reaches Lucas and Dar-Emmeline. Lucas's eyes are wide and watery, but Dar seems strangely calm.

She did this. I can feel it in my bones. A sudden rush of loathing shoots through every vein. Dar pretended to be my friend and companion and used me, and even now, after I helped her become whole again and protected her, she deceived and tricked me. If any harm comes to Lucas because of what she's done, I'll never forgive her.

The Lady stands before Lucas and Dar, smiling as if she is very pleased with herself. Her light brown curls shimmer in the sunlight, spilling out of her hood and down her back. She appears younger than Miranda, though not by much, yet I know she's ancient. When she speaks, her voice sounds like a melody. These tricks must be from talents she's harvested, though which ones I could not say. But perhaps it is how she puts people under her spell.

She leans close to Lucas and whispers in his ear. At first, he cringes and struggles, but within seconds he relaxes as a shadow falls over his face, stealing the light from his eyes. Then she whispers in Dar's ear too, and the same strange cloud befalls her.

"Come, my children," the Lady says, stepping back and regarding them. "You will join me in my garden."

Horror slides over my skin as Lady Aisling walks away—and my friends follow her, willingly, without a care in the world.

CHAPTER TWENTY-FOUR

With the help of Pearl, Cary and I return to our hiding spot in the ruins. But without Lucas, it feels as though someone has punched a hole in my chest.

Every speck of light, the sun and moon beaming overhead, are all reminders.

This is my fault. None of this would have happened without me.

As we arrive, we hear Noah calling out, his voice hoarse as though he's been at it for hours. We find him locked in the cellar of the main building with a gag loose around his neck. Dar tricked him early this morning, pretending to be me wanting to practice his talent.

The others begin to talk while I retreat into my shadows on the other side of the room. The darkness is a comfort, the only place I truly feel safe. I close my eyes, letting myself imagine what it would be like if I remained in the shadows for the rest of my days. I'd never be able to hurt anyone else if no one knew where I was. I'm sure my parents would agree that was best. After all, they believed I was dangerous and tried to hide me away. But then Lucas and Dar would still be trapped with Lady Aisling, and I'd never see them again.

My eyes flash open. It's my responsibility to fix this. I need to save them. Somehow.

As I release my shadows, Cary startles when I appear next to them, but quickly shrugs it off. They're all becoming accustomed to my appearances and disappearances now.

"Emmeline," Cary says. "Good, we need you."

Pearl pipes up. "Noah and I have an idea."

Noah smiles shyly. "I've been practicing."

"We both have," Pearl adds.

"What do you mean?" I ask.

"We need help. And a quick way to get it. What better way than recruiting the parents of the stolen children?" Pearl says.

"I've finally got my magic under control," Noah says. "I can hold it in for long enough for Pearl to shuttle me, and I can focus it to keep her magic away for nearly an hour. We were up all last night practicing, and it worked! I've been reading that history book of yours, Emmeline. If I concentrate harder, I might be able to do it for longer. Maybe even remove a talent permanently."

My eyes go wide. "Noah, that's wonderful news!"

"And then when we reach the bespelled parents, he can touch them, hopefully remove that spell, and then I can bring them all back here to regroup," Pearl says.

Cary brightens. "When we have the parents, we can march on Zinnia and force Lady Aisling to give up the people she stole. If that doesn't work, you can take us into the Garden of Souls, and we can use Noah's talent to set them free." For the first time since we found her, Cary positively glows.

Relief spills over me. If we can get the adults on board, it would be a huge help. Miranda and Alfred only told us a little about the network; these other parents surely know more and perhaps can call in reinforcements of some kind. At least they may have a better idea of what to do and can help us refine our plan.

"I think this might actually work," I say.

We gather round a makeshift table formed from fallen stone slabs, and I place the deeds of houses we visited on our journey here on the table.

"Start with my parents," Cary says with a determined glint in her eyes. "Please."

"Of course," Pearl says. "And mine next."

Another pang of loss shoots through me. If only we knew where Lucas's parents were, we could rescue them right now. I can't help wondering what my own parents are up to, and if they've all but forgotten me. Lady Aisling's henchman Lord Tate didn't need to resort to magic to convince them to give me up. But I can't worry about that now. I still have my shadows, and I need to help my new family first.

Maybe then I can go back and try to fix what happened with Lord Tate.

"All right," Pearl says, examining the deeds carefully until she has a clear idea of the location from the little map and what the place looks like from the drawing. "Are you ready, Noah?"

"As I'll ever be," he says. He holds out his hand and she takes it. Then she closes her eyes—*snap*—and they're gone. As much as I love my shadows, Pearl's talent has proved to be far more useful than my own.

Almost as soon as that thought circles my brain, I feel guilty for it, and wrap the nearest shadows close to me. They are loyal, and they are mine. I cannot regret them, not ever.

Cary paces the floor, anxious for her parents to return to normal, frantic energy leaking from her pores. Finally, she approaches me with a pained expression on her face.

"Could you…could you distract me?" she asks, wrinkling her nose. "I'd love to see more of your shadow weaving."

"Of course. It would help pass the time." I understand how she feels. I've gotten to know her better over these last few days. She struck me as tough and sullen before during our brief acquaintance in Parilla, but now I see it's more that she's fiercely loyal and protective. Just like an older sister ought to be.

I gather more shadows and begin to weave while we wait. First, I craft a puppy that rolls on the floor, chasing a shadow cat around Cary's feet. A small smile cracks her lips.

If Lucas were here, he could craft light to brighten her up

and blend with my shadows. I swallow hard, blinking back the tears that threaten. But he isn't here, and all I can do is amuse her as best I can with my darkness.

By the time I've nearly run out of shadow shapes to craft, a snapping sound breaks the quiet and Pearl and Noah appear out of thin air—and with them are the Rodans. Cary leaps to her feet.

"Mother! Father!" She rushes forward and throws her arms around each of them. For their part, the Rodans are dazed, but glad to see their daughter. Relief fills me, too; Noah's control over his talent is definitely improving.

Mr. Rodan frowns. "Where is Doyle?" he says. "These two said they would bring us to our family."

Cary's face twists, and she takes a step back. "You don't remember?"

Pearl and Noah stare at the ground uncomfortably. "We thought it would be best if they heard it from you," Pearl says.

The Rodans exchange a look. "Remember what?"

"The Lady."

Both of the Rodans' faces pale. "Oh no," murmurs Mrs. Rodan. "Tell us what happened."

"Doyle was taken, and the two of you were under some

sort of spell. You've been acting strangely for the last few weeks. Emmeline and Lucas came looking for Doyle, and I snuck away with them in the middle of the night."

"We suspect," I say, "that the spell Lady Aisling put on you allowed her to connect with you somehow, communicate if you saw any talented children. And she may have used a memory stealer to make you forget she was there. I'm sorry we snuck away, but we were scared."

Mrs. Rodan pulls Cary close to her. "You have nothing to apologize for. I'm glad you escaped if we were tainted like that."

"Where is Lucas?" Mr. Rodan asks, and now my face falls.

"He was captured. And so was Dar. We must save them both."

"That's awful," Mr. Rodan says. "His parents must be beside themselves. They've worked so hard all these years to keep him hidden."

"Who is Dar?" Mrs. Rodan says.

Cary raises her eyebrow at me.

I explain as best I can. The Rodans still frown, but to their credit they take my explanation in stride.

"Well, anyone who has fallen into her clutches needs saving. We'll have to figure something out."

"And we need to save Lucas's parents. That's how this all began. Miranda and Alfred were captured when she found our cottage by the sea."

Mr. Rodan slumps into a chair, and his wife puts a trembling hand on his shoulder. "That is the worst possible news. They're an integral part of the network. They're the record keepers."

"What does that mean?" I ask, my heart in my throat.

"It means that if Lady Aisling has them, she has everything. All the information she'll need to find every talented person ever hidden by the network."

CHAPTER TWENTY-FIVE

B y the end of the day, we have all the parents we've encountered on our journey free and ready to help, in addition to Cary's. Noah's parents were safe in their home when we found them, but they had had their memories altered just like the rest. It's a relief to have them all here to plan the best way into the city. We have been too much on our own for too long.

The best part about the adults being back to normal is they know more about the network than we do. While they are devastated by the news that Miranda and Alfred have been captured, we already have a plan to get them back: we march on

Zinnia at first light. My stomach is knotted with an odd mix of relief, guilt, and sheer terror at the prospect.

There is much commotion here in the ruins and questions to answer, but finally we manage to find time for some much-needed sleep.

It feels like I only blink, and it's morning again.

When I wander out of my corner, the first people I meet are the Rodans. Cary is with them, eager anxiety written all over her face. She's as keen to get her brother back as I am to free Lucas and Dar.

"Emmeline," says Mrs. Rodan. "We were just coming to wake you. We're almost ready." Together we walk outside the great hall of the ancient village. Mrs. Rodan will remain here to await Pearl and any talented people we set free. That way someone will be here to tend to the flowers and help them adjust if necessary.

I can't fathom what it would be like to be trapped as a flower for years and then suddenly be made human again. No one does, and we're prepared to help in whatever way we can. We know that some of her flowers have begun to wilt, but not what that will mean for them when they return to human form.

The adults will go in the main gates to demand an audience

with the Lady. The parents probably won't be able to force her to free anyone, but they will keep her and the guards busy while we circle back and sneak in through secret entrance Dar showed us. Then we'll follow the flowers to Lady Aisling's estate and her Garden of Souls. While none of us like the idea of leaving the adults at risk after we've just gotten them back, they insist it is our best chance.

With any luck, it will go as smoothly in reality as it does in my head.

After a quick breakfast, we set out. I keep Pearl, Noah, and Cary concealed within my shadows, a dark cloud trailing behind the group of adults headed for the town. The walk through the woods isn't far, but it feels as though it takes ages for the wall surrounding the town to come into view. When it does, my heart takes a seat in my throat, but I keep my shadows held tightly around us, protecting those in my charge.

Mr. Rodan walks right up to the main gate, two other sets of parents right behind him. A green-cloaked hunter stops them as they approach.

"Who are you, and what is your business in Zinnia?" the guard demands.

"My name is Stefan Rodan, and I am here to speak with Lady Aisling. We all are."

The guard glances at the guard next him. "And the Lady is expecting all of you?"

Mr. Rodan shakes his head. "No. But perhaps she should be."

The guards laugh. "Sorry, mate. If you weren't invited, you don't get to wander around our town looking for trouble. The people here love the Lady. It would not be a wise thing to do."

But Mr. Rodan holds his ground, as do the parents behind him. "We will not leave until we speak to her."

"Then you will be waiting a long time," says one guard. He holds out his sword in warning, and my heart begins to march double time. The argument between Mr. Rodan and the guards is beginning to attract attention. Townspeople stream out of the surrounding buildings and streets to see what the commotion is all about.

"We shall do no such thing," Mr. Rodan says louder than before.

"What do you want with our Lady?" one scowling man shouts from the crowd.

Mr. Rodan stands up straighter, making an imposing

figure. "She took my son. I'm here to get him back. She has stolen children from all of these people, and we will not stand for it." He sweeps his arm over the adults we gathered.

There is a sudden, strange shift in the demeanor of the townsfolk. As one, the crowd moves closer, almost like an orchestrated act.

"We love and honor our Lady! Anyone who does not isn't welcome in Zinnia!"

"We love the Lady! We love the Lady!" The chant rises like a tide through the crowd, chilling to hear.

There is no doubt in my mind these people are under some kind of spell. Noah touches my arm, fear on his face. I suspect he's realized the same thing.

"If they're spelled, I don't think I can cancel it on that many people at once." His hands quiver.

"Don't worry," I say. "It's time for us to leave."

The relief is visible on his face.

The crowd begins to shove forward as I lead the other children away. Our priority is getting to the garden and using Noah to release the talented folks trapped there; the adults will have to fend for themselves.

Once my shadows have slid out of sight of the main gates, we break into a run for the hidden door. Soon, we stand before it, breathless. I press the three places just as Dar showed us, and it swings open.

Then we step onto the path marked by the flowers that lead to the Garden where the Lady plants the flowers she prizes most.

CHAPTER TWENTY-SIX

ady Aisling's imposing estate rises before us. Intricate wrought-iron gates surround it, bordered by thick hedges that make it impossible to see through to the inside. The only glimpse we have is through the front gate—the sole entrance as far as we can tell—which reveals a long stone pathway lined by more hedges. A hint of a portico with large white columns flits through the foliage at the end of the path. The shadows here are intricate and deep, and they whisper around us in the breeze, tempting me to go inside.

Lucas and Dar and Doyle and many other victims are somewhere inside those hedges.

But finding the garden may not be as easy as I'd hoped. None of us have seen it, so Pearl can't hop there yet.

"Can you get us through the gates?" I ask Pearl. Any guards who were posted outside appear to have been called away to deal with the disturbance at the town entrance. Pearl gives a quick nod, and the four of us hold hands. I close my eyes as the strange tingling sensation washes over me, and when I open them again I'm looking through the other side of the gate onto the path where we stood only seconds earlier.

I use the shadows of the massive hedges to conceal us as we creep along the edge, hoping to find a way inside. The garden must be beyond the hedges, but it's impossible to tell how thick the foliage is. Noah furrows his brow beside me, concentrating as hard as he can to hold his nullification magic inside. I wish it wasn't such a struggle for him, though he is much better at it now than only a day or two ago.

Our plan is simple. Find the garden, use Noah to cancel the spell cast on each of the talented people planted there, and use Pearl to make a quick escape, all while my shadows keep us hidden. Hopefully once the flowers are free, it will be easier for us to find Miranda and Alfred and anyone else who may have fallen victim to her.

It all rests on our shoulders.

The weight of that responsibility bogs me down. I bear the blame in a way the others do not. I caught the attention of Lady Aisling's minions. I let Dar put her henchman in a coma. I ran away from home and straight into Lucas, putting them all at risk. I've lost everything I loved—my first home, my new home, my adoptive family, even my own shadow—through my foolish decisions.

But there is one person at the heart of it all who bears more guilt than I: Lady Aisling. At every turn, she takes and takes, devouring everything good in her path. I may only have one talent at my disposal, but I will use it in whatever way I can to defeat her.

We are halfway down the stone walkway when we first hear it: the sound of boots scraping against the stone. We shrink back as one, and I deepen and darken the shadows that surround us. We hold our breath as two green-cloaked guards march by on patrol. They are silent and stone-faced.

Once the guards are safely out of earshot, we move forward again. It is slow going, but we check every inch of the hedge on both sides of the path for any hidden entrances. I keep my eye on the sun's progress across the sky, the stubborn moon as unmoving as ever. It seems close enough to reach out and touch. It's well past noon, and as the day marches on toward evening, a chill slinks down my spine. If we fail here, what else will be knocked out of alignment in the heavens? I will the sun to move faster; the sooner the shadows descend around us, the easier it will be for me to keep us all hidden.

Finally, we reach the end of the long walkway and stand in the shadows beside a giant white porch with columns as thick as tree trunks. Many of them are carved to resemble trees, with interwoven branches and leaves forming the roof. Cautiously, we sneak between the columns, heading for the entrance to the estate.

The hedge continues all the way up to the red brick wall of the house. Our only way forward is through the front door. That on its own is a terrifying prospect. I have snuck into many places I wasn't supposed to be with only my shadows to hide me, but none as brazenly as this. My shadows hold fast, even though my hands quiver.

Being caught is unthinkable. For all of us.

Our little group hesitates, stooping beneath a wide stained-glass bay window next to the imposing double oak doors. Pearl peeks over the windowsill.

"The coast is clear," she says.

Pearl pops us into a huge room with shining mahogany

walls, intricate woven rugs, and paintings of gardens and flowers bursting with life. A sharp pang twists in my gut. It reminds me of the mansion I grew up in. Someday I'll have to return there to set things right and find a remedy for the man Dar put into a coma. But that all depends on succeeding here.

"We should split up," Cary says, "so we can cover more ground. This place is huge."

While I don't relish the idea, Cary is not wrong. The mansion appears enormous from where we stand. I don't see any windows along the far wall, only doors, so who knows how far back it extends.

"Pearl, Noah, look for the garden," I say. "If you find it, free as many as you can and get them out of here." I glance at Cary's determined face. "Cary and I will search for Lucas's parents and any other adults who have been taken, as well as Lucas and Dar."

Noah shifts from foot to foot nervously. "Do you really think that's a good idea?"

Cary stands up straighter, almost out of my shadows, and I quickly extend them to cover her. "It's the only idea if we want to find everyone."

Pearl shrugs. "We'll be safe, Noah. If anyone sees us, I'll just pop us away. I'm not worried."

Pearl and Cary's confidence in the plan makes me feel a little bit better. "Then it's settled. We'll go our separate ways and meet back here in an hour if we don't find anything." Assuming Lucas's parents are in fact here, and Lucas and Dar haven't been changed into flowers yet. The Rodans seemed to think Lady Aisling would keep them close and under her spell to make it easier to extract information from them as necessary. I shudder.

If the Rodans are correct, Lady Aisling already knows everything she needs about me and every other talented person hidden by the network. Miranda and Alfred were responsible for preparing new safe houses all over the three territories. That's why they had that list and all those deeds. It explains how Lady Aisling got to so many of them before us.

Cary and I take a left down one hall, hoping for a way into the lower levels of the house, while Pearl and Noah leave the safety of my shadows to go down the right-hand hallway. I hope Pearl has the presence of mind to pop away before anyone sees them should they encounter Lady Aisling or her minions.

We stick to the darkened corners and deepest shadows. We still haven't seen any windows, but there must be some at the back of the house. The paintings along the walls have gotten stranger, however. While the ones in the grand foyer depicted garden and pastoral scenes, these are of people.

People with talents.

They look old, perhaps from a time when talented folks were revered. We pass paintings of fire breathers, stone molders, shape shifters, green growers, and even a light singer like Lucas. They are vivid and lovely, but the eyes of each talented person are haunting, like they could see the future, could see what Lady Aisling had planned, and mourn the fate of their descendants.

We tiptoe past several rooms, peeking into each just in case, until we find a staircase nearly hidden in a shadowed alcove. Cary and I waste no time stepping into the welcoming darkness.

But something makes me pause on the first step—a rustling coming from the hall we just left. My heart leaps into my throat. Have we been found out already? I've been careful to keep my shadows secured, but perhaps Pearl and Noah ran into some guards. I put a finger to my lips and peek around the corner.

And quickly shrink right back.

I usher Cary down the stairs like a fire is at my back, desperate to get as far from that hallway as I can.

Because I saw the familiar dirty white dress of Simone. She is the last person I wanted to encounter here in Zinnia. Lady Aisling must have recalled her from the hunt after she captured Lucas and Dar, otherwise, I feel certain Simone would still be prowling the woods of Parilla and Abbacho.

I do not at all like the fact that she is roaming these halls instead.

I stop when we reach a landing to check no footsteps follow us down the narrow stairs. All is quiet and, for one moment, I feel safe here, wrapped in my shadows with a friend at my side. It's almost like the old days with Dar.

Dar, who is trapped somewhere in the mansion.

All that security drifts away like dust on a breeze.

Cary whispers to me, "What did you see?"

"Someone dangerous," I say, the only reply I'm willing to give just yet. "Someone we need to avoid if we want to remain undetected."

I motion to Cary to check the hallway on the right first.

It leads to a dead end and a locked door. Defeated, I turn away, but Cary touches my arm.

"I've always hated locked doors," she says. She pulls a pin from her hair and sticks it in the lock, jiggling, her ear bent close to the knob, until a soft click sounds. I suck in my breath sharply, praying no one is nearby to hear it. But our luck holds, and no guards appear to haul us away. Cary cracks the door open.

At first, it appears to be a normal sitting room with a couch and a plush chair set around a low table. That is, until I see the long, iron-barred cages against the walls on either side. Each contains a cot with a blanket-cloaked figure sleeping on it. These are definitely not guest rooms; this is a prison.

Cary frowns. "This is the strangest prison I've ever seen."

I shrug. "Perhaps Lady Aisling likes to interrogate people in elegant surroundings?"

"Or maybe she just wants to rub in how comfortable she is sitting pretty on that chair and how *un*comfortable those cells must be."

"Either way, we should free them. Anyone captured by Lady Aisling is a friend of ours."

As soon as the words leave my mouth, I realize how naive

they sound. Simone was captured by Lady Aisling. So was that boy and all the other shells she has under her control.

"But let's be cautious. Don't step out of my shadows."

We open the door a little wider so we can slip through. My hands shake as we tiptoe toward the nearest cage. It's dark with only one lamp lit on the table in the middle. Shadows are thrown every which way, but they are as familiar and friendly to me as my own hands. As we get closer to the cage, the person inside turns over, mumbling in their sleep. I stop short when the person's hair falls away from their face.

It's Miranda. Her dark hair, usually pulled back into a braid, is loose and unmistakable. Her skin is pale and sallow, and her eyes ringed by dark shadows, but there is no doubt it's her. The other figure must be Alfred.

At this moment, I should feel joy. We found them, after all. But all I feel is sick to my stomach.

"Miranda!" Cary hisses at my side. The sleeping figure blinks. In that moment real fear eats its way into my heart. Her eyes are wrong. Very wrong. I take a step back, dragging Cary with me as Miranda sits up.

Her eyes are entirely black, no whites or color at all.

She's under some sort of spell. What type and what kind of warning it might give to Lady Aisling, I do not want to stick around and find out.

Cary tries to throw me off. "What's wrong with you?"

"Look at her eyes. We can't stay here. We'll have to bring Noah back here to cancel it."

The sad prickling of failure creeps under my skin. This time Cary doesn't fight me as I drag her from the room. Footsteps echo above us on the stairs, igniting fear in my veins. Hurriedly, we take the left-hand corridor, trying every door we pass. When one opens I duck inside, Cary at my heels. The door closes just as a dark green cloak sweeps across the landing before turning down the other hall.

I settle into the corner by the door, crouched with Cary, trembling. Only when the footsteps march back up the stairs am I able to breathe normally again. Cary doesn't say a word, but her wide eyes are a reflection of my own.

Now that the footsteps have faded and my eyes have adjusted to the darkness, I take in our surroundings. It's a tiny room, furnished much more sparsely than any other we've seen in this mansion. A small bed with plain gray linens is pushed against the wall. A tiny sliver of a window peeks out onto green-ery at the top of the wall. It is unreachable even if we stood on the bed and no help in making our escape. In the opposite corner lies a closet where a slip of white gauzy fabric peeks out.

Something about that fabric is very familiar. Cary looks at me strangely when I get to my feet but doesn't say a word. I open the closet door, and my breath hitches in my chest. It is full of the same white gauzy dresses in varying states of dirtiness and disarray.

It's the same dress Simone always wears. This room belongs to her.

CHAPTER TWENTY-SEVEN

Though my brain insists I should be scared, curiosity gets the better of me. I examine the rest of Simone's room. I run my hand under the mattress—it's where I'd hide anything special to me—and find something thin and papery. I tug it out carefully.

It's a piece of paper, folded and unfolded many times over judging by the creases. I open it gingerly, not wanting it to rip.

Repeated enough times to fill the entire paper is a short list of names and places.

Simone Casares.

Parilla, Village of Wren.

Viktor and Romana Casares.

Violet Casares. Josef Casares.

Sorrow sinks into my skin as I fold the paper and replace it under the mattress. That must be the sum of Simone's past, or at least what she can remember of it. Written over and over as though that could imprint it on her memory. What did Lady Aisling do to make her need to do that? Is it a side effect of her magic or did the memory stealer we met have a hand in it? I shudder. While I don't miss my parents as much as I probably should, forgetting them entirely is not a thing I'd ever want to do. Like it or not, they're a part of how I became me, as much as my shadow weaving.

I hope when all this over, we will be able to find a way to help Simone, and the other shells too. The more I learn about her, the harder it is to leave her behind in this prison. But right now, she's working for the enemy. And while Noah may be able to reverse any spell, from what Dar said about Lady Aisling's talent, when it goes wrong it leaves damage behind. It may be caused by magic, but can canceling that magic fix it? I don't know the answer, and it's too risky to try while Lucas and Dar and many others are still waiting to be rescued.

"What was that?" Cary asks, breaking into my thoughts. For a moment, I almost forgot she was here.

"A cry for help."

"Someone you know?" She touches my arm, and I shrug.

"Only a little."

"Then we'll help them too. After Lucas and Doyle."

I smile faintly. "Thank you. But you're right. We must focus on your brother and our friends first."

With my shadows secured anew, we venture out into the hallway, a dark smudge on the walls, and make our way back upstairs with hearts a little heavier than they were before. But before we make it halfway up the stairs a new shadow falls over us, blocking the light and the way forward. My heart seizes as the shadows of several small figures march in our direction.

The shells are on the stairs.

We run back down, but at the bottom, three more children I recognize as shells from the market yesterday exit the room holding Lucas's parents.

We're trapped.

With nowhere to hide on the stairs, they will be on top of us any second. Cary casts around for something she can use to defend herself while I drop my shadows and weave them into tangible ropes instead to keep the shells at bay. The children close in, blank faced, moving almost as one. Could Lady Aisling control all of them at once like she did Simone, or is that how they always function when they're together? Without warning, they swarm us, though their expressions remain as frighteningly blank as ever. My shadow ropes snake through, catching some of them and constricting their arms to their sides, then tying them off in a tight knot. The shells struggle, but my ropes are strong and don't loosen an inch. But when I turn around to face the ones Cary has been holding off, I realize how quiet it has become.

Cary is gone, as are two of the shells.

Shock tears through me. I have no idea where they've taken her. She isn't talented; Lady Aisling won't want her for her garden. And the only other prisoners we've seen were right here. Frantically, I search every room with an open door and listen to the ones I can't unlock. There is no trace of her. None at all.

I race up the stairs, my shadows trailing after me like chains weighing me down. My breath is shallow and tight, and my hands sweat, making it difficult to grip the railing.

When I reach the top, there is no one in sight.

I fall to my knees in the alcove, hot tears sliding over my

face and silent sobs racking my chest. Another friend lost, and all because I couldn't help her.

A sudden burst of terror sends me back to my feet.

Pearl. Noah. I need to make sure they're safe.

I duck and weave back the way we came, leapfrogging from shadow to shadow until I'm in the entryway where we left Noah and Pearl. There's no sign of them, though I hear the echo of voices elsewhere in the mansion. I head down the hallway our friends took. It is brighter than the one we chose.

Up ahead there are windows. And beyond the glass, green.

The Garden of Souls. With any luck, Pearl and Noah are already canceling Lady Aisling's spells and spiriting away her victims. For the first time today, a glimmer of hope rises in my heart.

I make my way to a large room with whitewashed walls, marble columns, and huge glass doors that open onto the brilliant green of the garden. I slink along the walls, an unhinged shadow in a room full of bright hues and tones. The glass doors at the far end are cracked open, and I slip through, my pulse rising with every step.

My first sight of the Garden of Souls sends shock seeping through my veins. I knew there'd be flowers, but I never anticipated the sheer size.

They're massive. Giant versions of the familiar flowers I've seen in other gardens. No wonder this one is famous: sunflowers that stand twenty feet high, roses with enormous blossoms as big as my head, and stems as thick as a grown man's forearm. It is beautiful and terrifying at the same time.

I whimper. Lady Aisling's dangerous powers have not been exaggerated enough.

Please, please don't let one of these be Lucas or Dar. Not yet.

After checking for guards and shells, I cautiously step out onto the garden path. It winds in both directions, curling around beds of flowers and the odd wrought-iron bench and marble fountain. It is difficult to tell what might be hiding behind the next gigantic blossom. Near the outer hedges is a flower bed that must be the oldest part of the garden. It's a huge patch of zinnias. The once vibrant petals sag on their buckling stems. Some of the leaves are browning, and all are curled in like arms clutching their middles.

Cary was right—Lady Aisling's garden is beginning to die.

I back away from the wilting zinnias and head toward the main path. I don't have far to go before I hit gold.

There, in the midst of the garden, are Noah and Pearl. Relief floods my limbs like a cooling balm. They're safe. For now.

Noah places his hand on the petals of the nearest flower, and something magical happens, a sort of fizziness in the air. The petals—a gleaming white—begin to morph, pulling in closer to the bud as it sprouts eyes and a nose and a gasping mouth. Within seconds, the petals have transformed into a head and hair, and the leaves and stem are on their way to becoming legs and arms and a torso. Soon, a woman stands before us, gulping fresh air. Her hair is shockingly white, though she isn't old at all, and her crystal blue eyes remind me of ice. When she breathes out, I could swear I see frost on her breath even though it's a warm, sunny day.

The woman stumbles forward and collides with Pearl. Pearl catches hold of her and immediately takes them away to safety. Noah waves when he sees me step out of the shadows.

"I was afraid you might have been caught," he says, then frowns. "Where's Cary?"

I quickly explain what happened, and his face falls a little more with every word.

"I can't believe it. She's tougher than all of us, even without a talent." His face is as pale as the moon that still shines overhead.

"It's my fault. I should never have taken my eyes off her. I'll need you and Pearl to help get her back. I can't do it alone."

Noah stands up straighter even though his lip quivers. "Definitely." He scuffs his shoe in the dirt. "We've been trying to get through as many prisoners as possible, but there are just so many."

He sighs, and I realize he looks tired. I place a hand on his shoulder. "Why don't you sit over here out of sight and rest for a minute until Pearl gets back? Have you had anything to eat?" When he shakes his head, I rummage in my bag for an apple and hand it over. He takes it gratefully.

"How many have you and Pearl saved so far?" I ask. "Anyone we know?" The hope in my voice betrays me, but I'm sure if they'd found Lucas or Dar they'd still be here to help.

Noah's expression sours as he swallows a bite of apple. "Not enough, and no one we know yet." He sweeps an arm around the garden. The flowers nearest to him are the only ones where they've made a real dent. "Every flower here is a talented person. At least, that's our assumption. It's going to take forever to change them all back." He sighs. "We've saved maybe a dozen? But some of them were very old. It's hard to tell their age until they become human again."

"Lady Aisling has been doing this for a long time. She

uses magic to keep herself young. She may have only gone after children once she ran out of adults."

"No wonder there are so many of them here," Noah says.

"Dar is rather old too, since she's her sister. But she was stuck in an ageless limbo as a shadow for most of that time; it's not like she aged."

A sound pops behind us, and Pearl appears again, alone this time. "That one was so disoriented, it took me forever to calm her down and persuade her she was safe. I couldn't leave her alone until Mrs. Rodan joined us."

I wrinkle my nose. "What was wrong with her?"

"Nothing really, just disorientation. She's spent a huge part of her life as something other than human. What did you expect?"

"Did you find out what talent she has at least? Anything useful?" I ask.

"Maybe?" Pearl says. "She's a frost finder. She can make ice and snow. Nearly froze my fingers off taking her to safety."

Noah snorts. "At least she wasn't a fire breather."

Pearl glances around at the garden. "I'm sure there's one or two of those around here somewhere." She sighs. "All right, who's next, Noah?"

I relay the news about Cary to her while Noah swallows the last bite of apple and tosses away the core. The color is already returning to his cheeks.

"I don't think we should launch a rescue mission for Cary without talking to our parents," Pearl says. "They might even be able to get her back themselves. It's not like Cary is talented. She should be relatively safe."

I shake my head. "I don't know. Lucas's parents aren't talented either, but Lady Aisling did something terrible to them."

"I'm with Pearl," Noah says. "We should stick to our mission and then regroup with our parents. Besides, wouldn't Cary want us to keep going so we can find her brother?"

I swallow the angry retort on the tip of my tongue. He has a point. Cary would want us to find her brother and Lucas. "Fine. But we shouldn't stay still for too long. Those shells might come hunting for us here any minute."

Noah stands, his brow forming a deep V of consideration. "How about that one?" He points to the first flower in a nearby row of enormous petunias. I wander over to get a closer look, while Pearl rests on the rock he had been sitting on.

Noah stands in front of the flower, his hand about to touch

the stem, when something rustles behind us. I barely have time to turn around before hearing a woman's voice and the familiar *snap* of Pearl popping away to safety. My heart plummets into my feet, and I throw up my shadows.

I don't see Noah anywhere. Pearl must have taken him with her.

I only hope he can keep his talent under control. Random disoriented people wandering about the garden all of a sudden would give him away in a second.

I crouch low in the bushes, hoping whoever is coming is not the Lady and that they pass by quickly. But my hopes are in vain. A woman with long brown hair plaited down her back, rosy cheeks, and bright green eyes steps into view, and I suck my breath in sharply. There is no mistaking the mistress of the garden.

On one side of her is Lucas, and on the other, Dar—still bearing my form. She's brought them both here to make them part of her garden.

I can't sit here and wait her out. Not this time. I must do something.

But before I can decide what to do, another familiar face strolls into view, chasing my breath away. Simone, her unruly hair and dirty white frock the same as ever. Her eyes are wild and unfocused—right up until they fix on me.

Cold flashes over every inch of my body as the little girl smiles.

"I know you," she whispers, moving in my direction. I back up, concentrating on darkening my shadows as much as possible, but it is to no avail. Soon I'll have nowhere to go with the wall of hedges at my back and Simone advancing through the under-growth. I can hear the muffled sound of Lady Aisling calling to her pet.

"Simone, what have you found?" Something about her voice is both melodic and terrifying at the same time. I have no choice. I coil the shadows around my wrists, making them tangible and tacky, then send them soaring after Simone through the thick foliage. She squeals as they wrap tightly around her mouth, pinning her hands to her sides and her feet to the ground. She's trapped in the bushes now as much as I am. Lady Aisling can't see her through the thick leaves, but she may very well come after Simone when she doesn't respond.

I don't know where Noah is or when Pearl is coming back, but I can't wait any longer. I have to act now, or I'll get caught too. I burst from the shrubbery, shadows at the ready and twisted into a long rope that lashes out and winds around Lady Aisling, pinning her arms to her body.

At first, shock blossoms on her face, but then she laughs. It is a horrible thing that sends shudders down my spine.

"Well, one of you is not who you seem to be, clearly," she says, glancing between me and Dar. "We'll find out who you really are in just a moment." She turns her head to Lucas. "Lucas, would you be a dear and cut these ropes off me, please?"

Lucas's eyes are not normal. There's a dreamy expression in them, like his mind is miles away even though his body is present. He doesn't seem to recognize me. Instead, he sings, forming a ball of light in his hands. Then he molds it into something long and thin, until he holds a knife made of light. I gasp. That is far more advanced a thing than he's ever been able to accomplish before.

Lady Aisling must be controlling him somehow.

He uses the knife to slice through my shadow ropes, and my heart plummets into my boots. Lady Aisling shrugs them off and they scatter.

Then she faces me with her full attention.

CHAPTER TWENTY-EIGHT

Well, well, well," Lady Aisling crows. "Now, which of you is the real Emmeline?"

Dar cocks her head at the Lady, to all appearances under her spell. "I'm Emmeline, my lady," she says simply.

I try to speak, to contradict Dar, but the words choke in my throat. The temptation to let her take my place is strong—too strong. I immediately feel horrible. But lucky for my conscience, Lady Aisling is no fool. She glances between us again and laughs.

"I don't believe you. This one"—she points to me—"got past Simone and used a shadow rope to bind me. I have yet to see you use your magic," she says to Dar. "You can pretend to be something you're not, but you can't fake a talent. You either have it or you don't. And *she* has the magic of shadow weaving."

Lady Aisling examines Dar. "So," she says. "What exactly are you?"

Dar tilts her head. "I am Emmeline," she says again, confused. Has Dar managed to convince herself of this? Or is she faking it? I wouldn't put anything past her, but I also know how strong Lady Aisling's magic is.

"What about you?" Lady Aisling peers at me, seemingly unconcerned about whether I might escape. There isn't anywhere to run; I'm hemmed in by her and the hedges. "Do you know who she is?"

"I won't tell you anything until you release Lucas," I say, and the Lady laughs.

"Now why ever would I do that? He's mine now, aren't you?" She brushes a wayward strand of golden hair from Lucas's forehead, and he blinks at her slowly.

"Yes, my lady," he says.

"See?" She grins. "If you won't tell me willingly, then I'll just extract the information from you later. One way or another you will tell me what I want to know."

I clench my hands into fists. "Is that what you did to Lucas's parents?"

Lady Aisling smiles broadly. "Ah, so that was *you* sneaking around earlier with that girl, wasn't it? Yes, Miranda and Alfred have been quite helpful." She frowns momentarily. "Now, where did you tie up Simone this time? I'm sure she could be quite useful here. No matter, while Simone is a favorite, by no means is she my only pet." She snaps her fingers, and fear brews in my chest. "I believe you met some of them earlier?"

Footsteps shuffle on the path leading back to the mansion, soon followed by a line of vacant-eyed children walking toward us in single file. When they reach Lady Aisling, they fan out to further seal me in. I back away instinctively, knowing full well I have nowhere to run.

I call every shadow within reach, ready to defend myself. I will not be captured. I can't.

Lady Aisling glides over to a sunflower and plucks one of the petals. To my shock, she pops it into her mouth and chews it up, licking her fingers. When she swallows, the fizz of magic hums through the air.

Magic eater is a more apt name than I'd imagined. She

kneels and places her hands on the ground, closing her eyes in concentration. The air tingles with magic more potent than any I've ever encountered. I brace myself and my shadows, molding and shaping and readying for whatever it is she's about to send my way.

But her attack does not come.

Instead, her minions advance on me. At the head of them is Lucas. No hint of recognition lights his eyes.

My resolve falters, and my hands quake. The shells I am prepared to take on. But I can't fight Lucas.

I swallow hard as Lucas's light begins to take the shape of a brilliant flaming sword. He may not leave me much choice in the matter.

My hatred of Lady Aisling flares as bright as Lucas's light. She has taken everyone I've ever loved and poisoned them. This is the last straw.

The shells swarm, but I throw up my shadows around me in a bubble thick enough that they can't break through. For a moment, I give myself the luxury of taking a deep breath. The sun is dimmed under my dome, and even the brilliant moon seems to wane. But then Lucas advances, light sword raised high over his head. With one sweep of his arms and not a single emotion in his dead eyes, he slices through my shadows, making a door.

"That's it, Lucas. Emmeline is no match for you," chortles Lady Aisling.

I yank my shadows back, molding them into ropes though I know they'll be defenseless. While I may be able to make them tangible, they can't stand against the sharpness of light. When we work together, we're formidable, but being on opposite sides is a nightmare.

The shells pour forward, threatening to overwhelm me. Panic skitters over my skin. I don't know what they each can do, but I do know I can't let them touch me. That's how the memory stealer took one of Dar's memories. The others with mental talents may operate similarly. My shadow ropes snake through them, twisting around their middles and legs, sending them to the ground in a writhing mess of limbs and angry grunts. I pull the ends of the shadow ropes taut, then tie them off on the nearest hedge.

Lady Aisling's expression shifts to one of annoyance. "Lucas, you know what to do." She sneers as she raises her hands. The ground springs to life with thick vines that shoot up to wrap around my wrists, holding me fast.

Lucas advances again, holding the sword made of shimmering light.

My breath catches in my throat. In another setting, the weapon would be beautiful, possibly his finest work of lightcraft. But here…

The shadows in the garden wriggle out from between the gigantic flowers and wrap around Lucas's legs. They only slow his advance. He slices them away methodically, one side after the other, moving ever forward. I struggle against the vines, but it's no use. They've woven into my hair and around my neck. But still I send my shadows at Lucas, desperate to slow him, to talk him out of the Lady's spell.

"Lucas," I say. "Please. We're friends. Don't do this."

For a moment, he hesitates. Something new flashes in his eyes, then the light goes out again, and his face becomes as stony as before.

"You lied," he says. "You betrayed my family at every turn. You are no friend of mine."

The shock of his words slices into my chest, hotter and

more painful than his sword. My guilty conscience is mirrored in them, and the truth of it is heartbreaking.

"I'm sorry," I whisper. "I didn't mean to. I would do anything to take it back."

But he says no more, only tears through my shadows faster than ever. Then he stands over me, sword held high. Fear boils in my veins, and I struggle futilely one last time against the vines.

Behind Lady Aisling, Dar rises up, wearing the monstrous shape she favored and practiced for years as my shadow, now made flesh. Claws raised, wings spread, fangs bared, she howls.

And her sister turns.

Lady Aisling's pretty face twists with a mixture of surprise and recognition. She raises her hands as Dar lunges at Lucas, knocking him sideways and cutting through the vines holding me down in the process. I shove them off before they can recover. I hear a familiar soft *snap* somewhere nearby.

More vines snag Dar's wings and outstretched claws. The Lady yanks on them, and Dar tumbles forward, flailing her razor claws and slicing through the vines like a knife through butter.

It is all the distraction Pearl needs. She appears next to Lucas before he regains his feet, places her hands on his shoulders, and *pop*, they're gone. The tight band constricting my chest relaxes somewhat. She'll take him to Noah to undo the Lady's spell.

When the Lady turns around, her face is red and livid. "Not alone after all," she says. "Well, we can't have too many of your friends running around here, now can we? And to take my dear Lucas away so rudely. It shall not be tolerated."

Dar snarls at her sister as she gets to her feet, drawing the Lady's attention away from me.

"Darla?" Lady Aisling says with an admonishing tone. "Is that you? That monster looks familiar. And I've only ever known one shape shifter."

Darla. The name is an arrow in my heart. That's who Dar was before Lady Aisling did this to her. Before everything was stolen from her, she was simply a girl with a talent she loved. Just like me.

Dar springs to her feet and growls, her face taking on a feline visage as she settles back on her haunches and stalks around her sister in a circle. If I had everything taken from me like this would I be any different?

Lady Aisling begins to laugh. "Only you would be so foolish. Though I'll give you credit. Pretending to be Emmeline—don't think I've forgotten about you, dear—and to be under my thrall. Well played, dear sister, well played."

Dar lunges, but Lady Aisling is ready. Her vines wrap around Dar's neck, coiling over her body, and begin to squeeze. Dar thrashes, but the choking vines won't let up. I can't take it much longer.

"Stop it! Haven't you done enough to her already?" I cry.

The Lady glances at me but shows no sign of releasing Dar. "Oh, please. She had it easy. She knew what she was from the day she was born. For years, I hated her, thinking she was the twin who got all the magic. I spent so much time wishing and hoping for a talent, until one day we got into an argument and I was so angry I started shaking her. Her magic began to bleed out of her into me. I have fought to hone my talent ever since." She tosses Dar aside, but the vines continue their work. Dar's face begins to turn blue as her claws scrabble at her neck. She shifts into a smaller version of the monster, but the vines constrict even more.

Horror rolls over me, and I take an unconscious step back.

Lady Aisling laughs, believing me to be retreating. "I am much more adept at my powers now than I was when I first took Darla's. And there is plenty of room for you both in my garden."

CHAPTER TWENTY-NINE

Nausea steals over me suddenly, but I manage to hold it down. I will not let her hurt Dar. Not again.

As Lady Aisling grabs a petal from another flower and Dar continues to choke, I hear a pop, and then Lucas stands next to me. This time his eyes are not glazed over.

He is as furious as I've ever seen him.

Just as Lady Aisling swallows a new silvery petal, Lucas sings his light into a blade again and springs forward. He darts close, slices through the vines holding Dar down, then scurries back toward me before Lady Aisling has finished absorbing whatever her new magic happens to be.

We exchange a breathless glance, and a silent understanding

passes between us. We know what we need to do. Alone we are powerful, but together, we can do real magic.

Lucas and I pool our crafts. I can't help thinking about Cary's assertion that we need to use our talents to hurt—or even kill—Lady Aisling. The idea turns my stomach. I know it does the same for Lucas. What I don't know is how far Lady Aisling will push us. We're already close to the edge.

Dar screeches, her huge leathery wings beating as she rises into the air, then swoops at her sister. A geyser of water bursts from the ground, narrowly missing Dar: the Lady's new talent. Dar swerves midair and screams in response.

"You took everything from me! You condemned me to a half-life as a shadow."

"Your time as a shadow has only made you even more dramatic. If you come down here and play nice, I won't hurt you." Lady Aisling smiles sweetly at her sister, but it doesn't reach her cold eyes.

"I finally have my powers back. I will not let you steal them again. I won't let you steal them from *anyone* again." Dar circles and swoops, and the Lady sends another geyser straight for her. This time it pursues her through the air.

Lucas leaps into action, sending a beam of light careening into the geyser. It hisses, turning the water into mist and giving Dar the chance to get away.

Lady Aisling suddenly seems to remember we're still here.

"Now where did you learn to do that?" she says. "I don't think I've ever seen anyone make their powers so tangible as you two can. Except for me, of course."

"I showed him," I say, sticking out my chin. "I've shown all the talented people we've met."

She steps toward us, occasionally shooting spouts of water to keep Dar at bay. "You're more clever than I realized. How wonderful you'll soon be my pet too."

"I'll never be one of your flowers. And neither will Lucas!" A burst of my shadow ropes binds her arms and legs. It slows her pursuit, but it does nothing to halt her attacks on Dar. She must have eaten a petal from a water wisher—and I can't do anything to prevent what she does with her mind. When Dar dodges the latest surge, Lady Aisling tackles my shadow ropes, pounding at them with her water, wheedling underneath to pry them loose. Water always does seem to find a way through.

Moments later, she steps free of the shadow ropes, and my throat constricts with fear.

"I'm afraid you're going to regret that, Emmeline," she warns.

"What have you done with my parents?" Lucas cries, casting a blinding wall of light, forcing her to stagger back toward Dar.

The Lady only laughs. "They were very helpful."

"They're in the mansion," I whisper to him. "They're under her spell. We need Noah to free them."

Lucas swallows hard, but keeps a straight face. "Thank you," he says.

But the Lady isn't waiting around. Instead she traipses through her garden, holding Dar at bay easily and laughing, while grabbing fistfuls of petals from various flowers nearby. Soon she has a bouquet to form her arsenal of talents. My pulse throbs in my ears. I have no idea what we're in for, no clue what powers she holds in her hands and can absorb in mere seconds.

All I know is if we want to be free to live our lives, and to free those trapped here in her Garden of Souls, we're going to have to stand our ground and find out.

She swallows another petal, this one a brilliant red. I have a sneaking suspicion as to what that one does and make my shadows thick and strong. I cast them around us, weaving them into the wall of light Lucas creates. He sings more light into his hands, making a rope like the ones we used for Dar's cage. We are both thinking the same thing: if the cage worked for Dar, maybe it will work for her sister.

Lady Aisling's eyes glow red, and my knees go weak. She opens her mouth and flames spew forth, cutting through Lucas's wall. The light disperses, but he catches it again and adds it to the rope he's forming with his song. Dar settles on the ground, shifting before her feet even touch the grass. Her face grows wider, as do her shoulders, then her legs and torso thicken until she resembles a giant with skin as tough as a rock.

Lady Aisling sends a lancing flame toward her, but Dar simply shrugs it off. The Lady grunts with frustration, and Dar growls as they circle each other.

I whisper to Lucas, "We need to stop Lady Aisling, but we also need to contain Dar. She's dangerous when she's like this. Be ready." We may have made a truce with her for the other night in the ruins, but I'm not yet ready to trust her fully.

"We caught her once, we can do it again," Lucas says.

Lady Aisling yells as she lets loose another burst of flame, this one aimed at Dar's feet, the only somewhat vulnerable part of her body.

"But first, Lady Aisling," I say. Lucas's eyes glint.

"Now," I say to Lucas. Together we let loose our talents, light and shadow twining and bolstering each other in thick, braided cords toward the Lady and Dar. But the Lady sends flames at them, slowing them down and making the edges smolder, though not enough to stop them. She dodges and pops another petal in her mouth as guards arrive and march into the fray. We immediately focus our powers toward holding them back, Lucas with bands of light and me with my net of shadows. But they've gotten smarter since the last time we fought them and are better prepared. The first few I try to catch dodge out of the way faster than I can reorient my magic.

Frustrated, we keep at it, chasing the guards around the garden and keeping them away from Dar and the Lady so they can't give her aid, and they can't subdue Dar either. I wish it were night—if it were, I could use shadows to distract and disorient, but in the bright light of day, it would be too obvious what is shadow and what is flesh.

Lady Aisling summons her latest power—earth rattling—and stomps on the dirt. Dar is knocked flat on her back as the earth moves under our feet, and so are we. The guards stumble but must have experienced this talent before because they keep their balance.

Lucas and I scramble to our feet, light singing and shadow weaving at the ready. This time, my net catches them up a few at a time, and Lucas pins them to the hedges using his golden bands of light. No matter how much they struggle they won't be able to break free until night falls, or we let them go.

When we turn our attention back to Lady Aisling, she has Dar pinned to the ground and is sending jolts through her sister, laughing as Dar convulses, writhing in pain. We focus our combined magics on her, a burst of light and shadow sending her careening backward. I envelop her in shadows, making them thick and tacky and hard to move through, while Lucas uses hot bands of light to surround the shadows, encasing her. For one precious moment, Lady Aisling looks afraid before the light and shadow cover her face completely.

Dar groans, but regains her feet.

"What did you do?" she cries. "No! Emmeline, release her. I must destroy her myself! Please!"

"She's too dangerous. We can't risk it."

Dar howls, lunging for the shadow-and-light case surrounding Lady Aisling. She pummels it with her fists until they smoke from the heat of the light bands.

"Dar, stop! We've got her now, she won't hurt anyone again." Lucas says.

The ground quivers under our feet, but this time we remain standing. An awful wrenching noise follows. The sound is deafening, as if the earth itself objects to its power being trapped in shadow and light. Moments later, a crack appears in the garden floor, shooting across the ground.

The force of Lady Aisling's magic is rending the garden in two.

The crack widens. We leap back to avoid being swallowed. I hope Noah and Pearl are safely away.

The cage we created begins to crack, and then it implodes toward the center in shards of light and shadow.

Lady Aisling appears in the middle of the wreckage, sucking our magic toward her, until all the light and shadows we used to contain her disappear into her gaping mouth. She swallows and wipes her chin. Then she stalks toward us, arms raised and a ferocious expression on her face.

My hands go numb and my legs weaken. We've never seen anything treat our combined powers in such a way. She has been holding back, toying with us.

"You think you can contain me? I have unlimited powers at my fingertips." She inhales another shadow rope, and ducks to avoid Lucas's bolt of light.

"Not wholly unlimited," I say, stiffening my trembling chin. "You brought the Cerelia Comet back, didn't you? You did it because your Garden is beginning to die. I've seen it."

Lady Aisling's steps falter and surprise flits across her face for a moment before she regains her composure. "So smart, aren't you? I will enjoy devouring your powers."

Dar, still in her huge, rock-skinned form, screams and tackles Lady Aisling. The Lady's green silk skirts flare as they tumble to the ground.

Faster than a blink, Pearl and Noah appear next to where Dar and Lady Aisling tussle, close enough to the edge of the newly formed precipice to make my heart stick in my throat. Pearl hovers while Noah furrows his brow in concentration and grabs a lock of Lady Aisling's long hair just as she pops another petal in her mouth. The Lady's face shifts into strangled horror as she realizes she can't absorb the magic she just ate. Dar doesn't notice. Instead, she sprouts wings as she throws herself on her sister, yanking her off the ground.

Then Dar's face shifts too, and her body follows, changing back to the brown-haired girl I glimpsed the first time Noah accidentally touched her. The two of them careen over the sheer drop into the earth.

"No!" I cry. My shadow ropes, as thick as I can make them, shoot out. They wind around Dar's form, tethering her to the edge. Tentatively, I kneel to peek over the side.

Lady Aisling has also caught onto the shadow ropes, the two sisters too tangled up in limbs and skirts to separate. And both their talents canceled for the time being. Saving Dar means saving the Lady too.

"Let us go, Emmeline!" Dar pleads.

"If you let her fall," Lady Aisling says, "you're responsible for her death as well as mine. You don't want that, do you? Pull us up. I've seen your magic. Your ropes are strong enough."

I step back, hands shaking. I tuck them into my pockets.

"Don't do it," Dar says. "Let us both go. It's the only way to stop her for good."

How can I let Dar die? But how can I let Lady Aisling live?

"Noah," I say. "How long will it last?"

"A couple hours, I think." He glances nervously over the edge. "I'm sorry, Emmeline. I didn't realize it would affect Dar too."

I groan. "It isn't your fault. It must be because she touched her at the same time you did."

Lucas puts a warm hand on my shoulder. "Do you want to save Dar?" he asks with a serious expression on his face.

I know how he feels about her—pure loathing. She betrayed me, him, his family—everyone she has ever come into contact with. But she was my friend once. I can't help but want to save her. And she's already saved my life twice today.

I nod.

"I have an idea." He huddles with me and Noah, whispering his plan in our ears.

"You think it will work?" I ask.

"It just might," Noah says.

Lucas smiles. "We can do anything together."

"Save us!" Lady Aisling cries once again. "Save us, and I will give you anything you desire. You'll want for nothing. I won't plant you in my garden, I promise."

"Don't trust her," Dar warns. "She lies. She'd do anything to save her own skin. She'll just put you all back under her thrall the first chance she gets."

Dar is not wrong. When Noah's magic wears off, Lady Aisling will again be extremely dangerous. With a heavy heart, I begin to pull my shadows back. They snake toward me while Lucas readies his light magic and Noah concentrates, just in case. One nod, and our plan is thrown into motion.

Lucas sends two rings of light spinning out over the crevice, my shadows chasing after them and looping around each. One encircles Dar and the other lands over Lady Aisling's head. It slides down her body and pins her limbs to her side, forcing her to release Dar, yet catching her at the same time so she doesn't plummet. Now they're both secure and separate. But still hanging over the abyss.

With the help of Noah and Pearl, we begin to pull them up, Dar objecting the entire way.

Relief floods my limbs when we finally haul them over the edge. While Lucas secures Lady Aisling with light bands, I rush to Dar's side, my hands on her face, one that is somehow completely foreign and strangely familiar at the same time. But she does not welcome my embrace.

"How could you save her, Emmeline?" She scowls and shrugs away. Lucas dissipates his light and I my shadows, letting her move freely again.

She stalks to the other side of the garden, and I let her go. She won't be able to shift again for a while.

"I knew you wouldn't be able to kill me," Lady Aisling says with a smirk that makes the hair on the back of my neck stand on end.

Lucas glances over the edge of the rift. "I don't think you would ever have found your way up out of there," he says. "But I know we'd always wonder if maybe you survived. We don't need that hanging over our heads."

Lady Aisling's smug expression falters.

"Let me go. Or you will regret it," she says.

We all exchange a look. "We will take that into consideration. But first you must do one thing for us." I say. "Tell us what you did with the sky shaker."

She laughs. "Why? So you can put the comet back into alignment? I don't think so. I put it on a track to return yearly. I'll have plenty of new talents to harvest every year."

"That is where you're wrong," Lucas says, his hands balling into fists at his sides.

Noah steps forward, his brow furrowed and arm outstretched. Lady Aisling shrinks back, but can't go far with Lucas's light holding her fast.

"You wouldn't dare. You've already canceled my magic—are you going to keep this boy as my jailer, dampening my powers every few hours?"

I take a deep breath. This is the only way to ensure she can't hurt anyone ever again, but the thought of going through with it makes me nauseous. Noah hasn't had his powers long enough to fully understand how intrinsic they are to those of us who've had them for years. But Lady Aisling has made her magic a weapon, and she must be disarmed.

Noah places his hand on Lady Aisling's shoulder. "I don't know whether this will hurt," he warns.

"I hope it does," Lucas mutters under his breath.

We watch solemnly as Lady Aisling squirms under Noah's grip. But he holds on and concentrates harder than he ever has before. Within a few minutes, the familiar fizz of magic hums in the air, getting stronger every second.

Lady Aisling begins to thrash.

"What—what are you doing to me?" she cries. I wince but

Noah doesn't let go. He begins to lose the color in his cheeks from the effort. Finally, Lady Aisling goes limp, held up only by Lucas's light bands. A moment later a silvery mist emanates from her slack mouth.

Noah lets go and stumbles back. Pearl catches him. "I think it's done," Noah says.

I shudder. Lady Aisling is a magic eater no more.

CHAPTER THIRTY

N ow that Lady Aisling has been defeated, something unexpected happens. Throughout the garden, magic fizzes, released when the Lady's power extinguished. The garden begins to unravel. Blossoms become faces, stalks become bodies, and roots unfurl into legs. Soon every flower has been released and returned to his or her human form. It's a strange sight, the tall hedges now hemming in stone pathways and mounds of barren dirt instead of row after row of flowers. A few patches of grass, ground cover, and weeds are left behind, but not a single flower remains. The full breadth of Lady Aisling's evil, of the number of people she trapped here, the families she ripped apart, is stunning. Dar was not lying when she said Lady Aisling was very old and had been at this for a long time. She had years to hone her craft and put it to a most terrible use.

And now she'll never do that to anyone ever again.

We tend to the crowd of bewildered and disoriented people, but soon a clamor at the main gates catches our attention, and Pearl pops away to see what is going on. A few minutes later, she returns leading the parents we recruited, along with Cary.

"Cary!" I cry and run toward her. "You're safe! But how?"

She smirks. "Those shells don't tie knots tightly enough to hold me. It was creepy though. The two that were watching me just up and left at the same time without saying a word. But it gave me the opportunity I needed to get out of the cell. There's another level of them on the first floor farther down the corridor we were on."

"I'm so happy you're all right. Lady Aisling won't be bothering any talented people again." I quickly relay what happened.

"That is the perfect revenge." Cary glances around the garden. "Have you found my brother yet?"

"I haven't seen him, but he may be on the other side of the garden. Noah went that way to help them. I'd check there."

Cary immediately takes off after Noah, hoping to find her

brother among the restored talented folks. We haven't found the sky shaker yet, but we know they must be here somewhere.

Pearl approaches me and Lucas with a grin, the Rodans close behind her.

"You're not going to believe this," she says.

Mr. Rodan laughs. "We kept the villagers occupied as best we could, but it wasn't easy. Toward the end, they cornered us in the square. I thought we were done for certain, but then something wonderful happened."

"What?" I ask.

Pearl can't help grinning as Mr. Rodan continues. "They just stopped. Dropped their knives and staves and stared like they'd never seen us before. They had no idea what they had been doing only moments earlier. We knew something must have happened to Lady Aisling. She had them all under some kind of spell, but we didn't realize it would stop so suddenly." He looks around the garden in wonder as more and more people appear in place of the flowers, his eyes coming to rest on Lady Aisling's limp form. "So you did stop her, didn't you?"

Lucas's face is as grave as my own. "Noah destroyed her powers."

"The spell must have broken when her power disappeared," I say.

Pearl smiles. "Just like it did with the flowers."

"It's a very good thing we have Noah on our side," I say.

"She could still prove dangerous," Mr. Rodan says. "There is a prison in Abbacho where we can bring her. She won't be able to harm anyone from there." I glance over at where Lady Aisling remains bound by Lucas's light bands. She is still unconscious, but her hair is graying at the temples and her skin has begun to wrinkle. The removal of her stolen magic is catching up to her.

The parents mingle with the released talented folks, looking for lost loved ones and welcoming strangers back to the land of the walking and talking. Even though I know better, I can't help hoping that perhaps, somehow, my own parents were under a spell too. That was why they tried to force me to go with Lord Tate to be cured.

A scream goes up from the other side of the garden, but when Pearl pops me and Lucas there, we find Cary with her arms around a dazed Doyle. Tears prick my eyes.

Lucas pats him on the back, and Cary won't let go of her brother despite his squirming.

"Can you bring us to my parents?" she asks Pearl. "I know they'll want to see him too."

"Of course." Pearl reaches out to touch them both, then they vanish.

"You've made a lot of people happy, Noah." I say, and he blushes.

"I'm still trying to find the sky shaker in this crowd. But I've narrowed it down to the ones our age at least," he says.

Something sticks in my throat. We've worked hard to accomplish this, but we're not finished yet.

Pearl reappears beside us. "A lot of joyful people are out there. And among them are some you know. At least that's what the Rodans tell me. Come on," she says. Her hand brushes my shoulder. I blink and we're back to where Lady Aisling lays bound on the ground. Lucas lets out a cry of joy beside me and hurtles forward.

Miranda and Alfred stand next to the Rodans, free as birds and acting as though they're back in their right minds. Another familiar face—Alsa, the apothecary owner we ran to when Lady Aisling first appeared on our doorstep—peels off the crowd and embraces a woman who must be her long-lost daughter. Everywhere it seems families are being reunited.

I step forward, thrilled to see Lucas's parents, but I don't want to intrude on their reunion with their son. Miranda squeezes Lucas to her chest, then sees me standing awkwardly nearby.

"Emmeline!" she says, smiling broadly. "Come here." I join them, letting their arms envelop me. Hot tears of happiness spring from my eyes. I finally managed to put this right.

It isn't long before Pearl returns with Noah and the sky shaker, located at last. She is our age with wide gray eyes as big as saucers and hair the color of poppies. She introduces herself as Nova.

"Nova? Do you have a sister named Cheyenne?" I'm startled to realize that this is the very first talented person we arrived too late to find.

"I do," she says, distracted. She can't stop staring at the moon, so conspicuously out during the daytime. "The Lady did that, didn't she?"

"She did," I say.

Worry lines crease Nova's face. "My parents told me never to use my talent. Not ever. Once when I was little I brought a shooting star down near our house. Set the entire woods ablaze. It was so bad we had to move. They didn't need to warn me. I never dared use it after that. But why did she bring the moon out during the day?"

"She didn't. She brought the Cerelia Comet back twelve years early. That knocked the moon and a few other things out of alignment," Lucas says. "Do you think you can put them back?"

Nova nods hesitantly. "I suppose I'll have to try. If I put the comet back on track, that should fix everything else. At least, I hope it does." She shivers and wraps her arms around her middle, her shoulders curling inward. Then she closes her eyes and raises her face to the sky. For a moment, the heavens seem to shiver too, then stop just as suddenly. She gasps and opens her eyes. "It's done."

The moon has vanished from sight, and the remaining anxiety releases my limbs.

"Do you…do you know what happened to my family after Lady Aisling took me away?" Nova asks.

"They were bespelled, made to believe you were at a school for talented children. But they're safe now."

Pearl pipes up. "I can take you to them if you'd like."

Nova grins. "Yes, please."

My palms are sweaty as I approach Dar. She has fallen asleep on a bench, pale and wan, as though battling her sister took something vital out of her. Now that I have the full story of what happened between them and experienced Lady Aisling for myself, I understand Dar a little better. We have had our ups and downs, but I've seen the good in her between the darkness. Even as wrongheaded as she's been since she escaped, she still tried to help. She even saved my life. I have to believe it is who she was meant to be. I just want to be sure she agrees.

"Dar," I whisper. "Wake up."

Slowly her eyes flutter open. "Emmeline?" she says groggily.

I kneel next to her. "You look different now."

"You don't." Dar says, her shoulders drooping. Her talent has not returned yet. It must be eating away at her.

My heart hurts. Once we were literally inseparable. Close as sisters. Not anymore. But maybe we can heal the rift between us. At the very least, it's worth it to try.

To my surprise, Dar speaks before I do. "I'm sorry Lucas got caught by Lady Aisling. I never meant for that to happen." For once, she looks truly sincere. In fact she's been oddly calm ever since her sister lost her talent.

"Why did you switch places with Noah anyway? And why were those guards chasing you through the market?"

Dar sighs. "My plan was to sneak into Lady Aisling's estate while the rest of you were busy in the market. But I didn't get very far before the guards recognized Noah. I hadn't expected that."

I laugh. "Of course, they had captured him once, but we rescued him from their camp. You must have run into one of the guards from their search party." So she didn't betray us intentionally after all. That's a relief.

"I felt terrible that Lucas was caught. I couldn't let Lady Aisling take you too. That's why I took your shape."

"You were protecting me?"

Dar nods. "I promised you we'd always take care of each other. I meant it." She draws her knees up to her chest and wraps her arms around them. "What will happen to me now?"

"I don't know. What do you want to do?" Revenge has been the driving force behind Dar's every move for so long she seems a little lost now that it's complete.

She opens her mouth as if to speak, then shuts it again with a puzzled expression. "I never thought that far ahead before," she says. "But now... I think I'd like to stay with you. If you'll let me."

Hope dances across Dar's features, and I can't help but smile. "I believe we can arrange that."

She suddenly frowns. "But not in that cage. I need to be free. That's what I want most."

"Lady Aisling did a horrible thing to you," I say. "But now that her talent is destroyed, you have no more need for revenge. Do you want to move past this and finally be free of your sister?" I put on my best pleading look, praying that Dar agrees.

"Yes," she says. "I've been terrible to you. I couldn't see it before. I'm so, so sorry for everything I did."

Then she starts to cry.

I wrap my arms around her. She curls into my shoulder, sobbing. Dar sniffles and wipes her eyes. "I promise I'll be better this time."

"I believe you," I say and mean it.

Everyone deserves a second chance.

W e have spent the last week journeying back to Parilla—to my first home. Lucas, his parents, Noah, and Dar have all traveled with me. Before we left Zinnia, we set the network to finding the original homes of Simone and the other shells. Lady Aisling's power over them faded when her talent disappeared, but like Dar, the damage had already been done. They are free to act on their own again, but they'll never be the same as they once were.

Now there is one final thing for me to put right.

When we reach Parilla, my heart tangles in my throat. And when we finally arrive at the entrance to my parents' estate, my chest feels like it's been hollowed out. The mansion I once called home is so familiar, yet after all I've seen and done, it's also foreign at the same time.

It is the height of midday as we walk up the path to the front door. White brick walls rise in front of us, bleached like a skeleton in the sun. Vines creep over them, leaving restless shadows in their wake. I could grab onto them and shimmy up to my old room if I wanted to.

But that sort of entrance would not be well received.

Dar smiles encouragingly as we pause at the front door. Ever since her sister's powers were destroyed, she has been trying to make amends. This is the last wrong to set right: Lord Tate.

That fateful night when I agreed to Dar's assistance in changing Tate's mind and to help her become flesh in return is a bitter regret. It started everything. On the road here, she admitted she lied to me before: she cannot undo the damage done to him. She hoped to tweak something here and there to make him change his mind, but it was a foolish plan and not a thing she'd ever attempted before. As my shadow, a little of my talent bled off and left bits and pieces of shade inside him. Little did she know it would send him spiraling into a coma from which he might never awake. We searched Lady Aisling's estate for him but found no trace. But after we caught Alden, one of Lady Aisling's guards and Tate's nephew, hiding out in the town, he told me Lord Tate remained here at my parents' home. The doctors could not make heads or tails of his ailment and were too afraid to move him.

Noah came with us, too, in the hopes he can remove the magic keeping Tate comatose.

Miranda puts her hands on my shoulders. "We're right here with you, Emmeline."

They all know I'm terrified to see my parents again. They might refuse to even let me inside the house. I won't know until I knock.

Lucas takes my hand and nudges me toward the door. Together we lift the knocker and strike twice. The sound clangs in my ears; I never realized how loud it was. My hands quiver, and I clasp them in front of me.

The door opens, and one of the servants, Kendra, sees me on the steps. Her mouth drops open at the same time mine does. She recoils but doesn't think to shut the door on us.

Alfred speaks first. "We're here to see the lord and lady of the house. May we have an audience?"

Kendra manages to close her mouth and lets us enter the house.

"Just a moment, please, while I let them know you're here." She ducks away, no doubt thrilled to put distance between us.

A cold ache begins at the small of my back, worming its way up my spine. This is not the best reception. But what else can I hope for?

A few minutes later, rustling skirts alert me to my mother hurrying down the hall. When she reaches the atrium, she lets out a small cry. My father is right behind her.

"Emmeline! We were worried about you." My mother eyes the rest of our little company. "Who are all these people?"

A heady lightness washes over me. This is not at all the greeting I feared. "You were worried about me?"

"The last few weeks…months? Everything's been…hazy," Father says. "We're not sure what happened exactly."

"It was the Lady and the boy she brought with her," Mother says, her pretty brow creasing. "She arrived to evaluate her emissary's condition a few days after you ran off. She promised her guards would find you and would bring you to her school for talented children who wish to be cured. I don't recall much more than that."

"But a few days ago, everything changed," Father says. "It was like we'd been under a fog, and it suddenly lifted. That's when we found these strange letters in a drawer in my study. All of them exactly the same and signed by you. We knew something wasn't right. We sent runners to all the other noble houses in Parilla and Zinnia in the hopes they had heard something. But no one had."

I shudder as understanding courses through me. Lady Aisling bespelled my parents, even though I'd already run away. She even sent the fake letters to ensure they would never question what had happened to me. And she'd be free to steal my talent with no one the wiser.

"But now you're back," Mother says, tentatively placing a hand on my shoulder. Alfred and Miranda exchange a small smile. They know as well as I that this is more affection than my parents have shown me in years.

"These are my friends. Some of them are talented too, like me. You've been under a spell cast by Lady Aisling. That was the strange woman who arrived after I left, and the boy was probably her memory stealer. You can thank Noah"—I point him out—"for freeing you from her spell. And the rest of my friends for helping to defeat her. The cure you were promised was a ruse. She wasn't running a school, she was stealing talented children like me and taking their powers for herself. It was terrible."

My mother's face is aghast. "That is horrible." She releases her grip on me. "Emmeline, I am glad you're home. I don't remember much, but this big house was empty without you."

"I'm sorry we tried to send you away to be cured," Father says. "We had no idea what she was really doing."

Tears burn in the backs of my eyes. These are words I never expected to hear my parents say. "Thank you," I say. "I have so much to tell you. But first I must find Lord Tate. Is he in the same rooms?"

"Yes, he is."

We march up the stairs and down the hall to the guest wing, the old familiar shadows gathering at the hem of my skirt. We pass gawking servants who duck into alcoves and pretend they weren't staring as we pass. Have they been wondering what really happened to me and why my parents have seemed unconcerned? Lady Aisling's spell certainly explains why they didn't come after me right away. Only Lady Aisling and her hunters did.

The familiar guest rooms with their fine wall hangings and furnishings greet us, along with a doctor who regards us as though we have three heads each.

"What do you think you're doing?" He blocks our path into the bedroom. Lord Tate is just visible beyond him, a wan form lying limp in the guest bed.

"We're here to help," I say.

The doctor scoffs. "What do you think you can do? You're only children."

My father waves the doctor aside. "Let them try."

The doctor frowns, but steps aside.

Dar, Noah, and I enter, while Lucas and his parents remain in the doorway to give us space. Noah immediately grabs hold of Tate's hand, working his magic. He has come so far in using his talent, especially when he didn't know he had one not that long ago. But Tate does not wake. Not one eye flickers open, not one finger twitches. He remains exactly as before, chest rising and falling in shallow breaths, face pale as death.

Noah opens his eyes in confusion, releasing Tate's cold hand. "I don't understand," he says. "It's like I can't find any magic in him to nullify. But there should be, shouldn't there?"

Dar shrugs. "I don't know. I'm not entirely sure how I did it to begin with. All I know is that some pieces of shadow were left behind, and they're causing the problem."

I consider. "Perhaps the shadows were left behind, but no magic. And if that's the case, maybe I can help him after all."

I step forward, heart in my throat, clenching and unclenching my fists at my sides. I need to get this right. I'm Tate's last chance at ever waking up. Somehow I feel this responsibility most of all. It may have been Dar who did it, but it was my fear that gave her leave to try.

I close my eyes to focus on Tate. I call for the wayward shadows, every scrap that was left behind, to loosen their hold. Little by little, the tiny shadows respond. Soon, they whisper around my fingers like circling rings.

I open my eyes. And find myself staring into Tate's.

He blinks several times as his mouth hangs open. The doctor rushes forward as he realizes it actually worked. Dar bursts into tears, but all I feel is relief.

I may not have liked this man, I may have even feared him, but he can't hurt me anymore. Not with Lady Aisling gone. I'm glad he's been put right again, but I don't feel the need to remain here and indulge in boring conversations. I slip out the door, past my mother and Lucas and his family.

They let me go, sensing I need time alone. But Dar pads after me, knowing these halls as well as I do. Silently, we head for the kitchens, though they're empty now in the middle of the afternoon. A tray of lemon drop cookies cools on the counter, and I grab one just like I always used to do. For the first time, Dar takes a cookie of her own. Then we sneak out the kitchen door into the backyard, as we did a hundred times as girl and shadow. The sun is high over our heads, making the shadows short and sharp, but that doesn't matter right now. The woods beyond the field are dark and deep, and the only place we want to be.

I smile at Dar and take her hand. Eyes glistening, she smiles back. Then we break into a run.

ACKNOWLEDGMENTS

Every book is a new adventure with unique challenges and surprises, and *Comet Rising* is no exception. As I approached the drafting of this book, I (naively) assumed that I had it down (it is, after all, my fourth published novel—this whole writing thing should be easy now, right?). But while writing this book and promoting the first in the series, I was also experiencing being a first-time mom and working part time—all on a very tiny amount of sleep. I am infinitely grateful for the patience and flexibility of my excellent team at Sourcebooks and New Leaf as I worked through those challenges!

Particular thanks to the following lovely people:

My wonderful editor, Annie Berger, and the rest of the Sourcebooks team, especially Sarah Kasman, Alex Yeadon, Cassie Gutman, Stephanie Graham, Heidi Weiland, and

Valerie Pierce, for making my book shine and coordinating such wonderful events—it's a joy to work with all of you!

Suzie Townsend and Sara Stricker at New Leaf Literary & Media, for, well, everything. These books wouldn't have happened without you!

My husband Jason—thank you for putting up with my crazy schedule and being so supportive while we adjusted to life with a real baby in addition to book babies.

And last but not least, all the booksellers who have been so supportive of this series, and you, my readers. I hope you enjoyed spending time with these characters as much as I have!

ABOUT THE AUTHOR

———◦———

MarcyKate Connolly is a *New York Times* bestselling children's book author who lives in New England with her family and a grumble of pugs. Like the main character in her Shadow Weaver duology, she once had an imaginary friend who did very naughty things like eating directly from the sugar bowl and playing hide-and-seek with her parents—without telling them—whenever they went to department stores. Later in life, she graduated from Hampshire College (a magical place where they don't give you grades), where she wrote an opera sequel to *Hamlet* as the equivalent of a senior thesis. It was also there that she first fell in love with plotting and has been dreaming up new ways to make life difficult for her characters ever since. You can visit her online and learn more about her stories at marcykate.com.